I helped Duke pull the gate down, and then he asked me if I minded if he walked me down to 143rd Street.

"I don't mind," I said.

We walked all the way to the corner before he said anything. "You know, Cap is all right," he said. "But take a look at what happened today. Frank is talking about 'his case' and about how he didn't know this and didn't know that. The man's liable to end up in jail. Cap doesn't want you in Frank's shoes, and neither do I. Half the people in the world who find themselves in places they don't want to be in are going to tell you if they only knew then what they know now, things would be different. Frank's story is so familiar, I could have finished it."

"Maybe he just made a mistake," I said. "You can't help making a mistake sometimes."

"Jimmy, let me give you something to think about," Duke said. "You know how people manage not to do the wrong thing?"

"How?"

"By not letting themselves forget that they know the right thing."

ALSO BY WALTER DEAN MYERS

Fiction

IT AIN'T ALL FOR NOTHIN'

MONSTER
Michael L. Printz Award
Coretta Scott King Author Honor Book
National Book Award Finalist

THE MOUSE RAP

THE RIGHTEOUS REVENGE OF ARTEMIS BONNER

SCORPIONS
A Newbery Honor Book

THE STORY OF THE THREE KINGDOMS

Nonfiction

ANGEL TO ANGEL: A Mother's Gift of Love

BAD BOY: A Memoir

BROWN ANGELS: An Album of Pictures and Verse

MALCOLM X: A Fire Burning Brightly

NOW IS YOUR TIME!: The African-American
Struggle for Freedom
Coretta Scott King Author Award

Awards

*ALA Margaret A. Edwards Award for lifetime
achievement in writing for young adults*

*ALAN Award for outstanding contribution to
the field of young adult literature*

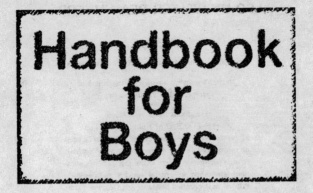

Handbook for Boys

A Novel

Walter Dean Myers

Drawings by Matthew Bandsuch

 HarperTrophy®

An Imprint of HarperCollinsPublishers

Amistad

Amistad is an imprint of HarperCollins Publishers

Harper Trophy® is a registered trademark of
HarperCollins Publishers Inc.

Handbook for Boys: A Novel

Printed in the United States of America. For information address HarperCollins Children's Books, a
division of HarperCollins Publishers, 1350 Avenue
of the Americas, New York, NY 10019.

Library of Congress Cataloging-in-Publication Data
Myers, Walter Dean, date.
Handbook for boys: a novel / Walter Dean Myers ;
drawings by Matthew Bandsuch.
      p.   cm.
Summary: Sixteen-year-old Jimmy, on probation for
assault, talks about life with three senior citizens in
a Harlem barbershop and hears about the tools he
can use to succeed in life.
ISBN 0-06-029146-X — ISBN 0-06-029147-8 (lib.
bdg.) — ISBN 0-06-440930-9 (pbk.)
[1. Conduct of life—Fiction. 2. Barbershops—
Fiction. 3. Harlem (New York, N.Y.)—Fiction.
4. African Americans—Fiction.] I. Title.
PZ7.M992 Han 2002   2001039505
[Fic]—dc21
                                                        CIP
                                                        AC

Typography by Alison Donalty
◆
First Harper Trophy edition, 2003
Visit us on the World Wide Web!

www.harperchildrens.com

For Mr. Irwin Lasher,
my sixth-grade teacher,
who made a permanent
difference in my life

Dear Reader,

I've lived long enough to see some of my childhood friends finish school, enjoy successful careers and even retire. Others I've seen end up in jails, or working far below what I had thought was their capacity. In looking at my friends, and others, I wondered what factors had led to their success or had been missing from their lives.

Some of the successes have been spectacular, but none have been as spectacular, in my view, as the failures. Speaking with young inmates is heartbreaking, especially when you see that they are often bright, articulate young people who should have done more with their lives. But if intelligence was not a major difference between success and failure, what was?

Over the years it became clear to me that people who did well were, almost without exception, actively involved in pursuing their dreams. Conversely, the people who failed most often were not involved in the process of effecting their own success. Many, in fact, did not even think they should have been involved. Success, they felt, was a thing of chance more apt to happen to those who had what seemed to be natural advantages.

There are teenagers who have fallen behind academically, don't see a way to catch up and stop trying. They often adapt to a lesser lifestyle, one far below their potential, and far less satisfying. At such times there is a desperate need for mentors, like the adults who frequent Duke's barbershop, but they are not often available.

I also see in my travels too many young people who sincerely want to succeed, and are more than willing to do the hard work to reach their goals, but who never get the information about life, jobs and values that they need to make true progress.

The advice needed by young people, whether it's given formally or informally, is best conveyed on a personal basis. This can be through the one-on-one mentor, the family experience or community organizations. I particularly love the idea of mentors, especially in those areas where there are not a lot of successful role models.

I know as a troubled teenager I would have loved to have had a neighborhood barbershop to sit in and a group of worldly and knowledgeable men to counsel me. Thinking about this was my motivation in writing this book, hoping it will be, in the least, a jumping-off point for many interesting conversations about success.

Walter Dean Myers

Contents

Handbook for Boys

A Novel

Prologue

"Mr. Lynch, you've been charged with assault on a fellow student, and you've admitted to the charges, is that correct?"

"Yes, sir."

"I have the authority, under the laws of this state, to assign you to a youth facility for six months. All it takes is for me to sign a form that my clerk will fill out and you'll be on your way. Do you understand that?"

"Yes, sir."

"Now there's a man here who has volunteered his time to help you straighten up. Mr. Duke Wilson is willing to take you into his community mentoring program for six months because he thinks, for whatever reason, that you're worth the effort. Can you give me a reason that I should put you on probation and release you to his supervision instead of putting you into a facility?"

"No, but I hope you do."

"I didn't hear you, Mr. Lynch. You didn't have any trouble speaking up when you were angry. Speak up now."

"I just hope you give me a chance, sir."

Duke's Place

The barbershop was on 145th Street, just off Seventh Avenue. They call it Duke's Place, but me and Kevin call it the Torture Chamber. Some people said that it was the oldest barbershop in the neighborhood, maybe even the oldest in Harlem. When I got there, I looked up at the wall clock and saw that it was three twenty-nine. I was early by one minute. Duke, who owned the place, was giving a guy a haircut. Mister M and Cap, the regular crew of old dudes, were already there. Cap was sitting in his favorite chair sipping on cold coffee like he always did. Mister M was reading *El Diario*, a

Spanish newspaper. Cap took his pocket watch out and checked the time and then gave me a mean look. I knew he was glad when I was late so he could get on my case. That was just the way the guy was made. He had probably been the meanest baby in the nursery.

"Hey, looka here." Mister M looked up from his newspaper. "They got this guy down in Georgia who's going to give away fifty million dollars. Man, some people just don't know what to do with themselves."

"What would you do with the money, Duke?" Cap asked.

Duke put the finishing touches on his customer's fade, then held up a mirror so the man could see how his haircut had come out.

"I'd put the money in the bank, down in the safe deposit vault," Duke said. "And maybe once a month I'd go visit it. Rub some all over myself till I got satisfied, then I'd put it all back until the next visit."

"Think you would move away from Harlem?" Cap asked. "Maybe go down to Florida or someplace like that?"

"You taking me out of Harlem would be like taking a fish out of water," Duke said. "I've got this place in my blood."

He took the money for the haircut and put it in the cash register.

"See you next month," he called after the customer.

"Wasn't that the guy who used to own the grocery store on Eighth Avenue?" Cap asked as the door closed.

"Yeah," Duke said, cleaning off his barbering tools. "Bill McCormick used to have that little piece of store on the corner until he started spending more time at the racetrack than he spent in his store."

Just then the door flew open and Kevin, sweating and puffing, came rushing in.

"Am I late?" Kevin asked, looking up at the clock that read three thirty-three.

"It depends," Duke said, "on whether you mean for today or for tomorrow. You're late for today, but you got a real good jump on tomorrow."

"Duke, you're wasting your money on this boy," Cap said as Kevin took off his jacket. "Your deal with him is that he's going to work for you after school for two years and you're going to pay his first two years of college, is that right?"

"That's right," Duke said.

"If he can't even tell time, how's he going to make it all the way through college?"

"Maybe he's fixing to learn how to tell time when he reaches college," Mister M said. "Even this ten-year-old boy knows how to tell time. What's your name again, boy?"

"My name is Jimmy, and I'm sixteen, not ten," I said.

"You got to keep them straight," Cap said. "Jimmy here's the young one. He's sixteen, and he's on parole from Alcatraz, or some place like that. Kevin is seventeen, and he's the one Duke is paying to get out of town."

Mister M cracked up on that. He's got this high laugh, and he slapped his leg like he was getting a big kick out of it. It wasn't funny to me. I started to say something, but when I looked over at Duke, he was shaking his head like he was disgusted, so I just kept my mouth shut and started dusting around the plants in the window. By this time Kevin had grabbed a broom and started sweeping the floor.

That's why me and Kevin call the place the Torture Chamber. Duke lets his old-time friends hang around all the time and stay on our cases.

I guess they were okay in their way, but

they didn't understand what being young was all about. Maybe they knew once, but they had definitely forgotten somewhere along the way.

Duke was tall and thin and always stood up straight even though he was sixty-eight years old. He told us he had gone to Storer, a black college in West Virginia, to study biology but ended up taking over his father's barber-shop business.

"When I was coming up, you had to take what opportunities you could find," Duke was always saying.

I had heard about Duke's studying biology at least a hundred times. That's where he had met his wife, Janice. She had opened a beauty school on 125th Street that she ran for a whole bunch of years. When she died three years ago, Duke sold the school and said he was going to use the money to send some kids to college. Kevin was supposed to be the first, and Duke said if I finished high school I might be the second. The first thing I needed to do was to finish the six months on probation so I wouldn't have to go to a youth house.

They called Edward Mills "Cap" because he used to work in the courts as a guard and always talked about all the criminals he had seen. Cap was about the same age as Duke. He and Duke met when they were playing basketball in a tournament back in the olden days. I didn't even know they were playing ball that long ago. Cap was a big man, mostly bald, and always looking like he was mad. Every day, rain or shine, hot or cold, he wore a vest and a bow tie. It was like his uniform.

Mister M's real name was Claudio Morales. Most of his life he ran a restaurant down on 142nd Street. When he retired from the restaurant business, he opened a little antique shop, which he hardly ever opened. He's not on our case as much as Duke and Cap but he's always laughing at us, and that can get on my nerves in a minute.

Duke's Place was never really dirty, but me and Kevin cleaned it the way we did five days a week. Kevin swept the floor and went over it with a damp mop. When I finished dusting the plants, I would clean the shelves and empty the ashtrays. All the ashtrays ever had in them were Mister M's chewing-gum wrappers. And all the time we were working, Duke, Cap and Mister M were steady on our case and enjoying it. When we left at five thirty, I was beat. Kevin asked me how my grades were coming, and I told him to shut up. I didn't need any advice from no brainiac wanna-be like him.

Kevin looked at me, shook his head and turned up Malcolm X Boulevard. I headed on home.

Kevin's mama had caught him smoking weed in his room and turned his sorry butt in to the police. She thought he was going to be a stone junkie or something. No lie. He was charged with possession and got ninety days but didn't do any jail time because of Duke.

My trouble came when I got into a fight in school. This guy moved into my space and started running his mouth about how he knew karate and what he was going to do if I didn't watch my step. We got into it and I wasted him. But then I was so mad that when it should have been over, I kept punching him. I knew it was wrong because he was hurt bad. His nose was broken and his lip was cut.

When the cops came to the house, I was still thinking it wasn't any big thing, but when they charged me with unlawful assault and started talking about jail time, I got scared bad.

When Duke got me out of it, I was glad as anything.

I had seen Duke around the hood and everything, but I didn't know him before he showed up in court. Duke was a dude you couldn't read that easy. He was like laid-back but not too laid-back.

"Just keep in mind that I'm on your side," he told me when we first met. That made me feel good about him.

I worked two hours every day and got paid on Friday. Part of the money went to Martin's family—that was the guy I beat up—to pay for his medical bills. What I got came to thirty-five dollars a week after taxes, and I was down with that. Kevin said that maybe Duke would work out a deal for me to go to college. I didn't go for it, because when people do things for you, they start getting all up in your business.

Kevin was a trip and I didn't like him that much. Before we got into trouble, I didn't even know him except I knew about him. He was one of those guys who was in the middle of everything. You start a club and he's the president of it. He was in the chess club, the photography club, and the choir. Big deal. I heard when he first got busted for pot, he was crying. He's my height, but he don't have no weight to him and I know I could put him on the ground if it ever went that way.

The money wasn't that tough, but I dug it because Inez, that's my moms, didn't have no whole lot of cash to be spreading around. She waits on tables in a diner down from the bus station on forty-deuce, and what she makes depends mostly on what kind of tips she gets.

"How did it go today?" she asked when I got home.

"I'm doing okay," I said. She was sitting on the couch with her feet up, and I could see her ankles were swollen. "You going to soak your ankles?"

"No, I'm going over to see Uncle Gilbert tonight," Moms said. "When I get back, maybe I'll soak them. You want to go with me?"

"No," I answered. Uncle Gilbert was really my mother's great-uncle. Moms thinks maybe he's losing it in the mental department. It was kind of funny, because he wasn't any older than the dudes in the barbershop but he wasn't nearly as sharp.

Me, I'm not getting old like that. I got my plans all worked out what I'm going to do with my life. That's what Duke is always talking about, getting a plan for living.

My plan is to play some ball in my senior year. I'm five foot eleven and a half. If I grow another two inches, which I will, then I might skip college altogether and join the NBA. Then I'm going to invest my money, maybe even open a restaurant and let my moms run it. Before I get as old as the guys in the barbershop, I can retire and just chill.

"How's Kevin doing?" Moms asked, putting on some lipstick.

"He's okay," I said.

"Come on over to see Uncle Gilbert with me," Moms said. "We can pick up some fried chicken on the way home."

I said okay because it wasn't that far and I didn't have anything else to do.

It was March, and the weather was warm one day and cold the next. Uncle Gilbert lived in the Robeson Houses across from the bus terminal. The Robeson Houses are cool, with a doorman and everything. I think Uncle Gilbert got some money somewhere, but he's always acting like he's broke. I didn't like him that much, either. It wasn't what he did so much but the way he looked. He looked a little strange to me, like he had some secret getover going on.

We walked to his place and took the elevator to the fourteenth floor.

"How you doing?" Moms asked when Uncle Gilbert opened the door.

"I got something for Jimmy to do," he said. Dude didn't even say hello.

"What is it?" Moms asked, digging her elbow into my side before I opened my mouth.

"There's a dog show coming to Harlem," Uncle Gilbert said. "I saw that on the television."

"That dog of yours can't win no dog show," I said. "He's not even a—what they call them?—a purebred dog. He's mixed up with two or three different kinds of breeds."

"First place you don't know nothing about dogs," Uncle Gilbert said. "If you did, you would have known Bailey is a girl dog, not a boy dog. And she can win if you teach her to do some tricks. I saw a dog in the movies once that could count up to ten."

I looked at Moms because I didn't believe what I had just heard. I must have heard it, though, because she had this funny look on her face.

"She barked out the numbers?" Moms asked.

"People teach their dogs to do tricks on television all the time," Uncle Gilbert said. "And since they're going to have a special part of the show for tricks, I think Bailey can win if you teach her how to count."

"I think that would be cute," Moms said.

"It ain't going to happen," I said.

"I'll give you ten dollars if you teach her," Uncle Gilbert said. "And if she wins the first prize of a hundred dollars, you can keep the money and I'll take the cup that goes with it."

"No way," I said. "Case closed."

Bailey is a scrawny little dog, and I wouldn't even walk it down the street. Half the dudes that got dogs on 145th Street got pit bulls. If I walked down the street with some punk-looking dog like Bailey, they would crack up. Next to them pit bulls Bailey wouldn't even make a good sandwich.

"If anybody can teach a dog to count," I heard Moms saying, "it'll be Jimmy."

On the way home she kidded me about how handsome I was going to look on television with Bailey when she won the prize and maybe my father could give me some pointers.

My parents are divorced, but a week ago my mom got a letter from my dad. He lives in New Jersey, only an hour and a half away, but he wrote a letter instead of coming by. She said he was making noises like he wanted to get back together with her. I asked her what she thought about it and she said it might work out.

"Things don't work out that easy," I said.

"Is that what they're telling you at the barbershop?" Moms asked.

"They don't have to tell me," I said. "All you need to do is to look around."

I know she didn't want to hear that, but as far as I was concerned, it was the truth. Another thing that was the truth was that I wasn't going to teach no dog how to count.

Victims

In gym I played some ball and I went up against Billy Ferris and tore him up. The coach saw me taking Billy to the hoop and asked me how come I didn't try out for the school team. I told him maybe I would next year. I didn't want to go into the whole thing about juvenile court and having to work in the barbershop. After gym, I took a long shower before I went to English. I was daydreaming a little and was still in the shower when the bell for the next period rang.

I got to English late, and Mrs. Finley instantly started flapping her lips. She asked me if I had done my homework and I said no. I was going to do it but I just forgot it and she got all uptight about that. The way she acted, you would have thought I dissed her mother or something. That one thing got my whole day going wrong. That's what a teacher can do to you. She kept going on about how I was wasting everybody's time and I told her she was the one wasting time messing with me instead of teaching English.

"What did you say, Mr. Lynch?" she asked. She started over toward me real slow. "What did you say?"

"I'm sorry," I said. I remembered that one of the conditions of my not going to a juvenile facility was keeping out of trouble. "I'm sorry."

By the time the last bell rang, I was exhausted. I was even glad to get to the barbershop.

The barbershop is like the center of the neighborhood. People gather around and talk and get all the latest news.

"This a place where men can gather and talk with everyone being equal," Cap said. "It's an American tradition."

"And the barber makes you look good," Duke said. He was cutting a little boy's hair.

The kid was checking himself out in the mirror and raising his eyebrow like he was being super cool or something.

"Hey, Jimmy, you retire or something?" Duke asked me.

"What do you want me to do?" I asked.

"Clean the tools," he said, knowing I didn't like cleaning them. He finished the kid's hair and told him the next time he saw him he'd have to trim his mustache. That was pretty funny, because right away the kid checked the mirror to see if he had it going on. He didn't.

Duke only used one set of barber tools. His set consisted of two electric clippers, two pairs of scissors, a pick and one razor. But when he said for me to clean the tools, he wanted me to clean all the tools in the place, which was four complete sets. I started cleaning them just as Pookie came in the door.

"Hey, Pookie, I heard you had struck it rich and moved to Saudi Arabia," Cap said. "You probably own two or three oil wells by now, don't you?"

"No, man, you're the one with all the money," Pookie said. "If I had your stash, I'd throw mine away."

He settled into the barber chair and closed

his eyes as Duke put the apron over him. Duke started picking out Pookie's hair, and just then Mister M came in with a bandage on his left hand.

"What happened to you?" Cap asked.

"Gabriela asked me to carry the laundry upstairs," Mister M said. "She had two baskets, one with whites and one with colors, and I didn't want to make two trips."

"So you piled one basket on top of the other and sprained your hand," Cap said.

"I lost my balance," Mister M answered, "and grabbed for a coat hook. Missed the hook and cut my finger on a nail."

"Was it rusty?" Cap asked.

"Naw, it was a clean nail. Just a scratch," Mister M said.

"Women will mess you up every time," Pookie said. "That's why I have to go downtown and get me a lawyer."

"What happened?" Cap leaned back in his chair. "Don't tell me you and your wife are having trouble."

"And the whole thing started over a chicken," Pookie said. "Now she's gone, I got my furniture out on the street and I have to get a lawyer to sue the landlord. It's a long story."

"It's early," Duke said, "and I don't have any place to go. What happened?"

"Well, it all started when Luvenia told me she was tired of staying home and watching television and wanted to go out more," Pookie started. "I told her that I didn't have any going-out money. I didn't know how serious she was. You know, some women complain just to be complaining. Anyway, she said she could stay home and watch television by herself and didn't need no man to help her do it. I told her that if she wanted to stay home, she should go on and do it and not bother me.

"The next thing I know, she's huffing and puffing and I'm sitting on the couch stuffing some potato chips in my lips because I ain't even watching where she going. You know what I mean? So then I ask her what she wants from me. She says she wants me to act more responsible, which, the way she figures it, means to take her out more. I know what she's getting at because I ain't nobody's fool. You know what I mean?"

"I know that," Duke said.

"So I get up and grab my hat, and I'm thinking of going to the fast food joint around the corner, next to the garage. But then I ask myself why I should spend all that money and let her think she making me do something. So then I roll over to the Pioneer supermarket and buy a chicken and bring it home and tell her why don't she make some fried chicken."

"You tell her or you asked her?" Cap asked.

"I told her!" Pookie said. "Luvenia tells me that maybe she'll fix the chicken and maybe she won't. So I put the chicken in the refrigerator. She thought I was going to get upset, but that's not me. I take things like they come. You know what I mean?"

"You showing her who's the boss," Duke said.

"Yeah. Anyway the refrigerator starts makes a clunking noise. Like *clunk! clunk! clunk!* She's been after me to get it fixed, but sometimes a refrigerator will make a noise for a while and then just stop all by itself. Ain't no use in putting out a whole lot of money every time it makes a little noise. So I'm sitting there not saying nothing and watching some television and the refrigerator starts making a noise like *clunkety-clunkety-clunkety*."

"How did it go?" Mister M asked.

"*Clunkety-clunkety-clunkety*," Pookie said. "Luvenia starts looking at me like I was making it do that. Then she asked me if I heard the noise it was making. Man, it was making so much noise that I couldn't hear the television. I told her, 'Yeah, I hear it.' Then she asked me what I was going to do about it, because she couldn't stand it making that noise all night long.

"I told her that if it was making that much noise, there was no use in fixing it because it was probably on the way out. That's when she really got her back up and said she was going down to see her mother in South Carolina and I could just call her when I got the refrigerator fixed or a new one. I told her that was just fine with me because I could make my own fried chicken and I would get the refrigerator fixed when I had a mind to get it fixed. She called down to the Greyhound bus company and found out when the bus was leaving for Winchester, Virginia. That's where her mother lives."

"She actually went to Winchester?" Duke asked.

"If I'm lying I'm flying!" Pookie said. "I guess she thought I was going to start whooping and hollering or begging her to stay. Anybody who knows Pookie Harris knows that

I take things the way I find them. I can deal with anything. So when Luvenia packed a bag and asked me for twenty-five dollars, I acted like I just didn't care. She went on out the door and I just let her go. Guess what. Guess what! *Just* like I said, *just* like I said, that refrigerator stopped making that noise. 'Round seven o'clock it stopped clunking and began to hum like it's supposed to do.

"She called me about eleven o'clock when she got down to Winchester, and I told her the refrigerator was all right just like I said it was going to be. She told me she was going to be back home in two days, which was going to be on a Wednesday, and I was to pick her up down at the Port Authority building because her mother was going to give her some jars of preserved fruits.

"So Tuesday comes and I get home from work and there's a paper on the front door saying I got twenty-four hours to leave the premises because they're going to evict me. I called up the landlord, and he says it's been three months since I paid any rent, and I had already told him that I was trying to get my car fixed because I needed a car to look for a job and as soon as I got myself together, I would catch up

27

on the rent. He got nasty and told me that if I didn't get down to his office in twenty-four hours with the money, he was going to take some action. I hung up the phone. You know, I don't think he's a citizen, anyway."

"Probably a foreigner," Mister M said.

"There you go," Pookie said. "We had four hundred and nine dollars, but I had to figure out what the landlord was going to do before I turned over my money. I didn't want to turn over our last money and then still get put out. I picked up Luvenia down at the Port Authority, and when we get to the house, there's all our stuff sitting on the sidewalk. Luvenia's crying and carrying on about what happened, and I told her it was her fault in the first place. If she had went on and made the fried chicken instead of carrying on so much, we would have been all right. She picked up her bag and headed right back to her mama's house. I'm living 'cross town with my brother. Ain't that something? All over some fried chicken!"

"It sure is," Duke said, putting tonic on the back of Pookie's neck.

When Pookie had paid for his haircut and

left, Cap and Mister M started laughing.

"Kevin, what do you think about my man Pookie?" Duke asked.

"I know he's never going to keep his wife if he doesn't take her out," Kevin said.

"He said he doesn't have a job," I said.

"Pookie is one of those people I call victims," Duke said. "He just goes from day to day, hoping for the best, and whatever happens, happens."

"He said he can deal with it," Kevin said.

"Yeah, but he has to deal with anything that happens to come his way," Duke said.

"That's what you got to do," I said.

"They don't put you out for being a few days late with your rent," Mister M said. "And if you're really late, they put a notice on your door so you can see it. He didn't have to deal with being put out of his house."

"Yeah, but he was right when he said the refrigerator was going to be all right," Kevin said.

"You can be a victim of good things, and you can be a victim of bad things," Duke said, easing down into the barber chair. "Pookie went through a little adventure. He had a little fight with his wife, which was bad. Not all that bad, but it was bad. His refrigerator is working, which is good. He doesn't have a job, which is bad. He got put out of his house, which is bad. He found a place to live with his brother, which is good. But who's controlling everything he's doing?"

"You can't know everything," I said. "The way you and Cap and Mister M talk, you're supposed to know everything in the world. Pookie come in here and he got to know about taking his wife out, he got to know about the refrigerator, and he got to know what his landlord is going to do. Nobody knows everything. And he's dealing with it. He didn't come in here asking anybody for anything."

"Jimmy." Duke had his eyes closed. "If you see a gang fight on the avenue, guys shooting back and forth, and you decide to walk past all the bullets, what happens if you get hit by one of the shots?"

"You might get hurt, and you might die," I said.

"But you have to deal with it either way, don't you?"

"Yeah."

"That's what Pookie is doing," Duke said. "Walking through the world with his eyes closed, and then talking about how proud he is of dealing with anything that comes his way. Sometimes a person has an accident or something happens that they can't avoid. They become a victim of that event. And then there are people who are victims all the time and just go from day to day to see what event they stumble into.

"Pookie knew he wasn't taking his wife out and she wanted to go out more. He knew he hadn't paid his rent. Those things wouldn't have happened to him if he didn't think like a victim."

"Which is what?" I asked.

"Which is I'll just go from day to day and see what happens," Duke said.

Me and Kevin swept the floor, and I straightened up the magazines and put the old newspapers in a plastic garbage bag. By the time I was ready to leave, Cap was busy telling Mister M how he should watch his hand in case it swelled up any and Duke had reclined the barber chair and closed his eyes.

When I got home, I did my homework,

including English; then I watched the North Carolina women play against Louisiana Tech. It was a good game.

"How did you like the spaghetti tonight?" Moms asked.

"It was okay," I said.

"Just okay?" She had her hands on her hips. "I made that spaghetti sauce from scratch, young man."

"It was good," I said.

"That's better."

"Hey, Moms, suppose I told you I was just going to go from day to day and deal with whatever happened?"

"Sounds okay to me," she said.

"That's what I think too," I said.

"Long as nothing too bad happens."

The Blind Monkey Strut

Sam's Fish Box is a restaurant right down the street from Duke's barbershop. They had a sign in the window saying they were looking for help. I went in and asked them how much they were paying, and Sam, who owned the joint, said he needed somebody with experience.

"To do what?" I asked. "To cook fish? All you do is put the fish in that wire basket and put it down in the oil until it's done."

"Don't be giving me any of your lip, boy," Sam said.

The trouble with adults is that they think they know everything and that if you're young you automatically don't know anything. Then when you show them you know something, they tell you not to be sassing them or giving them any lip. I didn't want the job at Sam's anyway. All I wanted to know was how much they were paying in case I did want the stupid job.

When I got to the barbershop, it was raining and Duke was rubbing his shoulder and talking about how it always hurt when it rained. Cap said that Kevin had called and wasn't going to make it.

"He's probably out robbing a bank," Cap said.

"Mister M isn't here," I said. "You think he's out robbing a bank?"

"Mister M's got a brain in his head," Cap said. "You got a brain in your head, you don't risk spending most of your life in jail."

The floor was dirty and a little damp, so I wiped it up and started looking around for something else to do when I saw Frank Greene coming through the door. Frank was a stone player. He was six four, and really knew how to dress. He was wearing a charcoal-brown suit, a yellow shirt, charcoal-brown tie, and dark-brown shoes. The brother was definitely fly.

"Mr. Greene, what's happening?" Duke got up out of the barber's chair so Frank could sit down.

"My case goes to the jury tomorrow," he said, settling into the chair.

"Your case?" Cap looked up. "What kind of case you got?"

"Man, I got caught up in a humble," Frank said. "Just give me a trim, Duke. I got to look good for the jury tomorrow."

"What happened?" Cap asked.

"It was a week after Christmas," Frank went on. "You remember when they kept predicting snow and it never snowed?"

"I remember that," Duke said.

"Well, I was down at the club I got a little piece of, and this dude comes in and tells me he needs some money to pay his rent and wants to sell his watch," Frank said. "I took a look at his watch and saw it was decent, so I gave him the thirty dollars he wanted for it. Didn't think nothing of it. Watch. Money. He split. I went back to my drink. You know what I mean?"

"No big thing," Cap said.

"Right," Frank said. "No big thing. Then in mid-January a detective comes knocking on my door, shows me his badge and asks me if I'm Frank Greene. I said I was, and he asked me if I knew what time it was. I look at the watch, and he says I'm under arrest."

"Under arrest?" Duke put his scissors down.

"Yeah. Seems they arrested some knucklehead on drug charges up in the Bronx. They go to this dude's house and find all this stuff he's stole. He's got televisions, guns, beepers and jewelry. Some of the jewelry was watches he boosted from some big department store downtown. Him and his brother's been selling this stuff to get money for drugs. And guess who his brother is?"

"Don't tell me he was the guy who sold you the watch?" Cap asked.

"The same guy!" Frank said. "They picked this guy up and charged him with every unsolved burglary in the city of New York and two from New Jersey. Then they asked him where the other stuff was. He told them who all he sold the stuff to, and they went out looking for it. The only one they got was me, because all the other people he sold stuff to were junkies, and they traded it for dope."

"All you had to tell them was that you

didn't know it was stolen," I said.

"The boy got something there," Cap said.

"That's just what I told them," Frank said. "But you know, here I am, a black man who's got his stuff together, and they snatch me off the street and take me downtown. I'm on trial along with this fool's brother for dealing in stolen goods, man. Ain't that a crock?"

"It's not right," Cap said, shaking his head.

I knew Cap was going to have some more to say after Frank left.

"So, what's the watch worth?" Duke asked.

"They say it's worth about a thousand dollars," Frank said. "All I know is I was trying to help the guy pay his rent. If I had known he was a thief, I wouldn't have even talked to him."

"I hear you," Cap said. "You sure can't tell a thief by just looking at him."

"That's exactly what I'm going to say at the trial," Frank said. "Yo, Duke, let me put this on my tab."

"Sure," Duke said, taking the apron off Frank. "You're looking clean, man. The jury will see that."

Frank checked himself out in the mirror, nodded approval and left.

"What you think, Jimmy?" Duke asked. He was brushing the hair off the chair that Frank had sat in.

"I know you and Cap are going to have something to say about it," I said. "Anybody can make a mistake, but you figure everybody should be perfect. You're not even perfect."

"You're probably right," Duke said. "But let me ask you something. You ever hear about the Blind Monkey Strut?"

"You know I never heard anything about no Blind Monkey Strut," I said.

Duke sat in the barber's chair, reclined and folded his hands on his chest.

"There was a monkey walking through the jungle one day when he saw a big 'Help Wanted' sign nailed to a tree. Being a curious kind of monkey, he went over to see what it was all about. The sign said the tiger was look-ing for somebody to teach the Monkey Strut to his children and they were paying off in bananas. Now the monkey had never heard of the Monkey Strut, but like I said, he was a curi-ous kind of monkey, so he went and asked the tiger what he had in mind.

"'I'm looking to teach my children to get along with everybody here in the jungle,' the tiger said. 'And the best way of doing it is to teach them how to do the Monkey Strut. You know, the way you monkeys strut around so proud and everything. I'm willing to pay two bananas a day, too. Of course, if you teach the Blind Monkey Strut, I'll pay fifty bananas a day.'

"The monkey scratched his chin and asked the tiger exactly what he meant by the Blind Monkey Strut. The tiger told him it was the same thing as the Monkey Strut except you did it wearing a blindfold. Well, that didn't sound that hard to the monkey, so he signed up for the job. The tiger gave him a blindfold, and he put it on and started strutting around.

"'Strut over here!' the tiger called.

"The monkey strutted himself right over into a trap the tiger had set, and before you know it he found himself hanging upside down all tied up while the tiger started lighting up the fire under his pot in preparation for eating the monkey. While the tiger was putting some curry and plantain leaves in the pot for seasoning, another monkey came by, saw the monkey upside down in the tree and asked what happened.

"'The tiger hired me to teach the Blind

Help Wanted
teach the monkey
stray ƒor my kids
- earn bananas
- tiger

Monkey Strut,' the monkey wailed. 'If I knew when I first came along what I know now, I would have taken the two bananas!'"

"'You knew tigers eat monkeys,' the second monkey said. 'You didn't need to know anything else!'

"And that's the story of the Blind Monkey Strut," Duke said.

"What's that got to do with Frank Greene?" I asked.

"Frank knows a thousand-dollar watch when he sees one," Cap said. "And he knows nobody is going to sell him a thousand-dollar watch for thirty dollars if it's legitimate. What else did he need to know?"

"He wasn't sure if it was stolen," I said. "The guy didn't say it was stolen."

"Jimmy, tell me something," Cap said. "How many bananas a day do you work for?"

"You don't have to diss me," I said to Cap. "If I said something like that to you, I'd be wrong, but you can say it because you can get away with it."

"You think Jimmy's mad, Duke?" Cap asked.

"Sounds like it, Cap," Duke said.

I didn't say anything else for the rest of the

day. When it was time to go, Duke told me to help him pull the gate down because he was closing up early.

Cap said he would see us tomorrow, and Duke said good-bye, but I didn't say anything. If Cap was my age, I would have been upside his head and he knew it.

I helped Duke pull the gate down, and then he asked me if I minded if he walked me down to 143rd Street.

"I don't mind," I said.

We walked all the way to the corner before he said anything. "You know, Cap is all right," he said. "But take a look at what happened today. Frank is talking about 'his case' and about how he didn't know this and didn't know that. The man's liable to end up in jail. Cap doesn't want you in Frank's shoes, and neither do I. Half the people in the world who find themselves in places they don't want to be in are going to tell you if they only knew then what they know now, things would be different. Frank's story is so familiar, I could have finished it."

"Maybe he just made a mistake," I said. "You can't help making a mistake sometimes."

"Jimmy, let me give you something to think about," Duke said. "You know how people manage not to do the wrong thing?"

"How?"

"By not letting themselves forget that they know the right thing," Duke said. "When most people do something wrong enough to get them into trouble, they know in their hearts it was the wrong thing to do but tell themselves they really don't know it. Those bananas looked good enough to the monkey for him to forget he was dealing with a tiger. That watch looked good enough to Frank for him to overlook the idea that it was probably stolen. Think about that."

"Yeah, okay."

When I got home, Moms was making fried pork chops and Uncle Gilbert was sitting at the table going through a dream book.

"Help your uncle look up the number for losing teeth," Mom said. "I already know what it means. If you dream about somebody losing teeth, it means there's going to be a death in the family. Hope it's not somebody close."

"I don't know how you can believe in that superstitious stuff," I said.

I looked under false teeth and saw the number next to it, 0-6-5.

"That's as good a number as any other,"

Uncle Gilbert said, writing it down in the little notebook he always carried around with him.

"Say, Uncle Gilbert," I asked, "what's the worst mistake you ever made?"

"Worst mistake I ever made?" Uncle Gilbert rubbed his chin with his fingertips. "I had a little piece of land down in Chambersburg, Pennsylvania. All I had to do was pay the taxes on it, but I let it slide and let it slide. Then my cousin told me they were building around there, and I went down to see about it, but the county had taken it over for back taxes and I lost it. Could have made some nice money on that land if I had kept up the taxes."

"How much were the taxes?" Moms asked.

"About thirty dollars a year back then."

"How far were you behind?"

"I never did pay the taxes, so it must have been eight years or so before they took it," Uncle Gilbert said. "That's according to my cousin, anyway. You remember Cousin Fred, don't you, Inez? Long head, had a mole on his chin?"

"Yeah, I remember him," Moms said.

"You didn't know you had to pay the taxes?" I asked.

"I knew it but it wasn't no big thing," Uncle Gilbert said. "If I had known then how much land was going to go for, I'd have kept them up. Why you ask?"

"Just wondering," I said. "That's all."

Does Life Work?

I was surprised when Duke called me on a Sunday afternoon. He asked me if I had done all my homework. I didn't have any homework over the weekend, and I told him. He asked if my moms was home.

"You don't believe me?" I asked.

"I believe you," Duke said, "but I'll believe you even more when your mama tells me it's true."

I put my mother on and he asked her. Then she gave me her "You'd better not be lying to me!" look and I told her I didn't have any home-work. Then Duke must have said something else to her, because she was nodding her head up and down.

"Just a minute," she said, putting her hand over the mouthpiece. "You want to help Duke move a friend of his today?"

"Yeah, I guess."

When I got back on the phone, Duke told me he had to move a friend of his from 147th Street over to 145th near Broadway. He gave the address and told me to be there at two thirty. He didn't mention anything about money, but I knew Duke—he didn't expect people to work for nothing.

When I got there, Duke was sitting on the stoop. He had the keys and started explaining what we had to do as we went up the stairs to the apartment. Some regular movers were going to come by in the morning to take the furniture, but me and Duke were going to take his friend's collection of plates. The apartment was small and neat, and I could tell it was an old person's place because he only had one small television set and that sat on top of a chest of drawers in the bedroom.

"Where's the dude?" I asked.

"Billy's in the hospital," Duke said. "He'll be out tomorrow or Tuesday, and I want to get him straight so he can move right into his new place."

"All we're going to move are some plates?"

"And we're going to try not to break any of them," Duke said. "Billy's been collecting these tea sets for years."

I saw the tea sets—there were a dozen of them, tiny little cups, saucers and sugar bowls that looked like they would break if you gave them a hard look.

"How come you're moving him?" I asked.

"Billy's okay." Duke had brought some boxes and newspapers with him, and he started taking the tea sets from the dresser, wrapping them up in the paper and putting them carefully into the boxes. "I've known him ever since he moved to 147th Street after he got out of the army and opened up his laundry. When he closed his laundry a few years ago, some of his people wanted him to move down to Chinatown, but he decided that all his friends were here in Harlem, and so he stayed up here."

"He's Chinese?" I asked. "I thought you said his name was Billy."

"He's got two names," Duke said. "He's got a Chinese name and an American name.

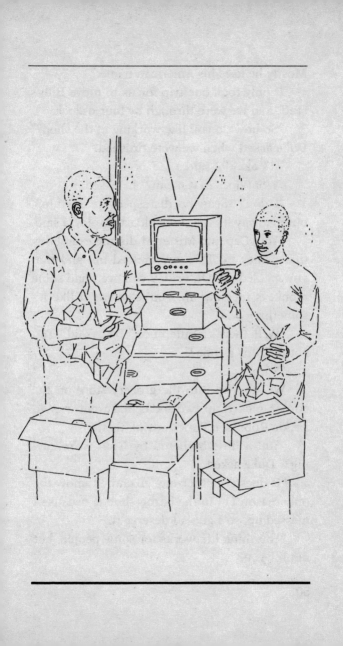

Mostly he uses his American name."

It only took one trip for us to move Billy's stuff, and we were through by four o'clock.

"So how do you like working at the shop?" Duke asked when we were finished.

"It's okay," I said.

"What does that mean?" he asked.

"I don't mean no disrespect or anything, but in a way it's the same old same-old," I said.

"You, Cap and Mister M dissing everybody that comes in. This guy messed up, and that guy messed up. On Friday you even had some monkeys messing up. You're saying it like it's something new."

"Well, there's a difference," Duke said. "You got time for a soda?"

"Sure."

We stopped into the grocery store on the corner, picked up two sodas and went over to Jackie Robinson Park to drink them.

"You a little bothered by what we're saying?" Duke asked.

"It doesn't bother me," I said. "I know the only reason I'm in the barbershop is because I messed up, so I guess I deserve it."

"You think life works for some people, but not for you?"

"I'm no different than anybody else who walks into the shop," I said.

"Yes, you are," Duke said. When he drank his soda, his Adam's apple went up and down and looked funny, but I didn't laugh. "Most of the people who come into the shop never talk about things we're talking about. They're not talking about if life works, or what works and what doesn't."

"Nobody talks about that stuff except you guys," I said. "They don't even talk about all this stuff in school."

"Philosophers spend all their lives talking about the same things we're talking about," Duke said. "They write big books on the subject. There was a guy who spent years thinking about life and finally came up with what he thought was a really great idea. He knew he had been thinking and thinking for all that time. So then he figured if he was thinking, then he had to exist. He said, 'I think, therefore I am.'"

"I am *what*?"

"Just he *was*," Duke said. "He knew something had to be doing the thinking, and he knew he was doing it, so he had to exist."

"He was lame, right? I mean he couldn't

just look at his hand and see he was there?"

"Look, Jimmy, no matter what we talk about in the barbershop, it doesn't make sense that half the people who walk in there are busy messing their lives around, does it?" Duke asked.

"You want my answer?" I asked. "Or you want Cap's answer?"

"Well, give me both," Duke said.

"According to Cap, everybody's going down the tubes," I said. "And according to me, some people are blowing their thing and some ain't. You know, I can't see dissing everybody."

"Neither can Cap," Duke said. "But check out those kids over there. They got their little lives together, right?"

I looked over to where Duke was pointing and saw two little girls building a house out of cardboard. There was a little boy with them, and he was trying to get a toy truck into the house.

"Yeah, they look cool," I said.

"Cap knows that they're cool, too," Duke said. "But he also knows that little boy might end up in the court system, or in jail one day. And he wants to know why, and I want to know why, and you want to know why."

"I want to know why?"

"Don't you?"

"Yeah, I guess so."

"So what's the first question you're going to ask yourself?"

"If he ends up in jail or something like that, I guess I'd have to ask what he did wrong," I said.

"How about: Why would he do something that was wrong in the first place?" Duke asked. "By the time he's nine or ten, he's certainly going to know right from wrong."

"I don't know why he's going to do something wrong," I said.

"But if you don't know why he's going to do something wrong, and he's such a good-looking young man, playing nice with his little friends and all, how are you going to know if your children are going to do something wrong?" Duke asked. "How do you know if you're going to do something wrong?"

"How about this?" I said. "Before I bust a move, I'll come by the barbershop and have you and Cap check it out."

"So you'd be willing to take my values and Cap's values and apply them to yourself?" Duke asked.

"That could work," I answered. "Least

you guys ain't in jail."

"So you find somebody you respect, check out their values, and then use them as a role model." Duke nodded to himself. "I like that. But suppose that little brother over there sees his neighborhood drug dealer, with his bad machine all shiny at the curb, a fist full of Benjamins and two fly hootchie mamas on either arm and thinks that looks pretty good? What would you say to him?"

"How fly are the hootchie mamas?"

"Uh-oh, they got you, too?" Duke raised one eyebrow.

"Okay, I guess we're supposed to get down to where we say something about figuring out right from wrong and how we're going to do the right thing," I said.

"No, we're supposed to get down to where we begin to wonder what exactly is right and wrong," Duke said. "When you talk about the easy stuff, there's nothing to think about. If I ask you how many drugs you should take this week, or how many banks you should rob, you can give me a quick comeback. But that little boy over there is not going to wake up one day and decide to become a crack head.

54

And when they have a career day in school, he's not going to put down how he wants to be a stick-up man.

"If he goes wrong, it's going to be a lot of little things that nobody is even going to notice," Duke said. He had finished his soda and took it over to the trash can. I had put mine down under the park bench but snatched it up right quick and took it to the can, too. "Then one day, if he goes wrong, and I hope he doesn't, he's going to find himself doing something that's even going to surprise him and wonder how he got there."

"So all the little brother has to do is to remember a thousand things about what not to do and he's straight, right?" I asked.

"Well, me and Descartes were thinking that it's a lot more complex than that," Duke said. He started walking toward the park exit, and I went with him.

"He hangs out in the barbershop, too?"

"Descartes? No, he was the one who said, 'I think, therefore I am,'" Duke said. "Me and Descartes think that you have to figure out for yourself how you should live your life. You need to sit down and think it all through until you get it settled in your mind, and then live it. We figure if you think hard enough, and you start with the fundamental questions, you'll get it right."

"So what you got figured out?" I asked.

"So far I've got two things figured out," Duke said as we got to the car. "Get in and I'll drop you past your house. By the way, did you go to church this morning?"

"No, man, I slept too late."

"Okay, I see we're going to have to get Sister Smith talking to you about that. Anyway, like I said, I've got two things figured out," he went on. "The first thing is that life doesn't work. The second thing—"

"Whoa! Whoa! Did you say that life don't work?"

"No, I said it *doesn't* work," Duke said. "If life worked by itself, all you would have to do is wake up every morning and be an interested spectator on how your show is working. You can look around you and see that's not happening."

"It looks like it's working for some people," I said.

"No, life isn't working for them," Duke said. "They're making their lives work by figuring out how they want to live and acting in their own interest. It's like a basketball game. Does the game work, or do you have to make it work?"

"I got to think about it," I said. "What's the other thing you got figured out?"

Duke pulled out of the parking space and then had to stop quickly when a dude on a skateboard cut in front of us.

"That one of the main reasons people get themselves messed around is that they reach a point at which they become spectators in their own lives," Duke said. "People get discouraged, or sometimes they don't know what to do, and just stop being players."

"How long it take you to figure that out?" I asked.

"Most of my life," Duke said.

"And how old is that other dude?" I asked. "The guy who said *I think* and stuff?"

"Descartes? He died about three hundred and fifty years ago," Duke said. "And he's still one of the most important philosophers who ever lived."

"Well, I'm glad you didn't spend no whole lot of time with him," I said. "I still think he was kind of lame."

"Maybe. But if I had my way," Duke said, "I'd start every little boy in Harlem in prekindergarten philosophy, let them start thinking about how to live their lives when they're three and four years old, not when they're in the back of a police wagon."

"What you would have is a whole bunch of little pains in the butt," I said.

"Are you saying I'm an old pain in the butt?" Duke gave me his pretend mean look.

"You know I wouldn't say something like that," I said.

Duke gave me ten dollars for helping him move Billy, and that was cool. He really didn't even need me to help, but I guess he just wanted to talk to me some more. I wondered if he didn't have anything else to do on Sundays since his wife had died. I also thought about all the little kids in kindergarten listening to him and taking courses in philosophy.

When I got home, Moms was making supper and doing a crossword puzzle at the same time. She asked me if I knew a five-letter word that meant "contest place."

"I can't think of that right now," I said. "I just learned today that *I am.*"

"You are what?" she asked.

"Just *I am*," I said. "I also learned that life doesn't work."

"Maybe not," Moms said. She had breaded shrimps sizzling on the stove and turned them over with a spatula. "But it do beat dying."

Does Life Work? Part II

"**Just the** same way I used to hate the Yankees in the old days, I love them today," Cap said. "If they win every game for the rest of the year, I would just love it dearly."

A customer came in with a girl and asked Duke if he had any black shoelaces. He was decked-down tough and had gold in his mouth. His girl had on a tight, short little dress that she kept pulling down. Duke told me to get some laces.

I looked over in the case and found two boxes of black shoestrings. One was for three-hole shoes and the other was for four-hole shoes. I checked out the customer's shoes, saw that they had three holes and handed over a pair.

"How much I owe you?"

"Fifty cents," Duke said.

The man pushed a hundred-dollar bill over the counter. Big deal. I showed it to Duke. He looked at it, held it up to the light, and then made change.

"That's all I got with me," Mr. Goldteeth said with a little grin. He gave me a dollar tip and walked out the shop with Miss Tightdress wriggling right behind him.

"Nice we got such big men in our neighborhood," Cap said. "Just imagine, some guys don't have nothing but hundred-dollar bills in their pockets."

"You need hundred-dollar bills to keep that chick," Kevin said.

"He could have bought her a dress that covered more of her legs than that," Duke said. "At least me and Jimmy think so. Ain't that right, Jimmy?"

"I guess he just wants to show her off," I said. "Like he wants to show off his gold."

Mack came in. Mack got some hair on the right side of his head and a little on the left. He doesn't have anything on top and not much in the back. He still comes in once a week to get it trimmed.

"Big Mack, how's it going?" Duke asked.

"Man, I am as mad as I can be," Mack said.

"It's not like you to let things get to you," Duke said. "What happened?"

"I'm walking down Malcolm X Boulevard, down near 135th Street this morning," Mack went on. "Just when I'm passing the library there, this guy comes up to me and says, 'Hey, brother!'"

"And you're telling me that he wasn't your brother?" Cap asked.

"He wasn't my brother and he turned out not to be a friend, either," Mack said. "He asked me if I had any spare change. I was about to tell him to take a long walk off a short pier when I started thinking that I was standing in front of the library for black culture and history. Okay, so I wanted to give this 'brother' a break. I reached into my pocket and pulled out fourteen cents. When I handed it over, this guy threw it down on the ground."

"He didn't want your fourteen cents?"

"He said I was an old, bourgeois punk!" Mack said. "I walked on up the street because he was acting crazy as far as I was concerned. Then he come up behind me and said I should give him a dollar, because it cost a dollar to get something to eat.

"I figure everybody is entitled to three square meals a day and a warm place to live. But I don't think that they are entitled to curse and scream at me because I only had fourteen cents in spare change."

"He cursed, too?" Cap asked.

"Yeah, he cursed," Mack said. "I don't want to say everything the guy said because there's kids around. He called me every name in the book. Some I have never heard before."

Duke shook his head. He was trimming Mack's hair, which mostly meant making noises with the scissors because, as I said, Mack didn't have that much hair.

"Mack, do you really think that this guy was entitled to three meals a day and a warm place to live?" Duke asked.

"Yeah," Mack said. "I guess so, but I don't think that he has the right to ask me to get it for him."

"Kevin!" Duke called to Kevin, and Kevin, who was daydreaming, jumped. I liked that, because Kevin gets away with daydreaming all the time.

"What?" Kevin asked.

"What do you think everybody is entitled to?" Duke asked. "Mack says three meals a day and a warm place to live. What does Kevin say?"

"Nobody should be hungry," Kevin said. Then he looked right at me.

"What you looking at me for?" I asked him.

"He's going to ask you next," he said.

"I haven't finished with you yet," Duke said. "Is everybody entitled to three meals a day?"

"Why not?" Kevin said.

"So if I get you right," Duke said, "just because a person is born means he's entitled to a few things. Let's say, just for the sake of argument, that the person in question doesn't choose to work for anything. All he wants to do is to sit on the stoop and watch the world go by. Is he still entitled to his meals, and his place to stay?"

"Most people will work if they have a chance," Kevin said.

"I know what you mean," Duke said, "and I certainly agree. But this particular person

we're talking about today is kind of an odd
duck. He wouldn't work as a mattress tester.
He wouldn't work as a sniffer in a perfume factory. He just does not like work. Period. Case
closed. Is he still entitled to his three meals a
day and a place to live?"

"Yeah, I think so," Kevin said.

"And who's entitled to pay for his three
meals?" Cap asked.

"And when the landlord comes around
looking for his rent, who's going to come up
with the check?" Mack asked.

"If the government didn't waste so much
money, they could pay for it easy," Kevin
answered. "They collect enough taxes."

"Let's say," Duke began again, "that everybody east of the Mississippi River decided that
this not working was a good deal. They all
decided to sit out on their stoops and listen to
the radio and pass the time of day in friendly
conversation. Then, according to you, everybody who lives west of the Mississippi should
chip in and pay more taxes so that people on
the east coast can have what they're entitled to?"

"Now you're hyperbolizing!" Kevin said.

"I'm what?" Duke put down his scissors.

"You're hyperbolizing," Kevin said again.

"You know, blowing things out of proportion."

"Good thing this ain't a small shop," Cap said. "Or a word like that wouldn't even fit in here."

"Jimmy, can you give us the benefit of your wisdom without using words that are going to give an old black man a headache?" Duke said.

"I don't want to talk about it," I said.

"What I don't understand is why that guy thought *I* should give him my spare change, which I worked hard for, so he could get on with *his* life," Mack said. "I bet if I asked him to go to the store and get me a cold soda, he wouldn't do it."

"The people who run the world have things set up for themselves," Kevin said. "The way they've got it figured out, they're all going to get over. So they're taking money and making bombs and planes and starting wars and stuff, and they're all getting over like fat rats. All I'm saying is that the little guy should get a break too."

"That's a good point," Duke said. "Jimmy doesn't want to speak on it, but I'm sure he thinks things should work out so the brother at least gets him a sandwich."

"I want to know what kind of menu are you

going to put out for those three meals?" Cap asked. "Are we talking about steak or are we talking about beans and rice?"

"It doesn't have to be anything fancy," Kevin said. "But it should be enough so that people aren't hungry."

"Pork chops?" Cap asked.

"Man, that doesn't matter," Kevin said. "The point is that people should be able to eat!"

"It matters to me," Cap said. "If I'm feeding you out of my taxes, then I want to know what you're eating. And to tell you the truth, if you're greasing down on steaks, mashed potatoes and gravy and I'm eating somebody's nasty leftovers, I'm not going to take to it too kindly."

"Whatever," Kevin said.

Duke tried to push it more, but Kevin wasn't going for it, and I knew I wasn't going for it, either. So then they started back into talking about baseball again like it was nothing to it. By the time Mack left, he wasn't even thinking about the brother who had asked him for some spare change.

I got home and asked Moms what she was entitled to from life.

"I'm too tired tonight, Jimmy," she said. "I'll think about it tomorrow, okay?"

"Sure," I said. I was a little disappointed, though. I knew where Duke wanted to take the conversation. If life worked, he was going to say, then everybody would automatically get their three meals a day with no sweat. It didn't happen that way. A lot of people were hungry big-time and down and out big-time. But just because life didn't work for everybody the way I thought it should, it didn't mean it just didn't work at all.

Another thing I was wondering about was: How about the brother with the hundred-dollar bills and the hot sweetie by his side? Life was not only working for that brother, but it was working big-time. One thing I was sure of was that Duke was going to bring the subject up again, and when he did, I had some hard questions for him.

Duke Talks About Success

When I got to the barbershop, only Duke was there. He looked up at the clock.

"Early today?"

"We got out a little early," I said. "So I thought I'd come over and figure out who's messed up their lives today."

"You can learn a lot from people who do well," Duke said. "But you can learn from people who don't do well, too. The funny thing is that when people do mess up, they usually do it in a way that you can see fairly easily. Success is more subtle. Sometimes you look at somebody who's done well for themselves and it's hard to see why."

"Are you successful?"

"I've done okay," Duke said. "I could have done better, I think."

"If you had known then what you know now?"

"Now, wasn't that a nasty thing to say to an old man?" Duke was grinning. It was the first time I had ever seen him with a big smile on his face.

"I just wondered what you were going to say," I said as I picked up the feather duster and started dusting the stuff in the window.

"Well, it's about learning," Duke said. "I did a lot of things right just out of balancing my common sense with my fear. If I had sat down and thought out the whole thing when I was your age, I could have directed my success a little better."

"You said you were balancing your fear?" I looked at Duke to see if he was kidding me. "What were you scared of?"

"Lot of things," Duke said. "I was scared of going to jail, so I kept myself straight. I was scared of getting into too much debt, so I never

71

did owe that much money out. I was scared to tell my daddy I wasn't going to go to college when he told me I was going to go, so I got a fairly good education. All that helped."

Just then Cap and Mister M came in carrying a fish tank. The tank had sand in it and a little castle, but no water. They put the tank near the window, and Cap went over to where he always sat.

"If we get a fish that looks as smart as Jimmy here, I'm going to put him next to the checkerboard," Cap said. "Maybe I can teach him the game."

"Jimmy, I think Cap is saying you can't play no checkers," Mister M said.

"I'm not worried about what Cap is saying," I said.

Kevin came in just as the clock on the wall hit three thirty. He said something lame and grabbed a broom. His eyes were a little bloodshot, and I wondered if he had been drinking or something.

"Jimmy said he's tired of hearing about losers," Duke said. "He wants us to tell him how to succeed, get rich and marry a movie star."

"You want to hear a success story?" Cap

asked. I turned and saw he was pointing at Mister M. "Listen to this man right here. Go on and tell these young boys how it's done."

"Where do you want me to begin?" Mister M asked.

"Were you born in a log cabin?" Kevin asked.

"When you reach his level of success," Cap said, "then you can make your little jokes. Until then you'd best try to learn something."

"I was born in Ciales, Puerto Rico," Mister M said. "My father worked picking coffee. Then we moved to Caguas, and my dad worked for the same guy he had worked for in Ciales. In Caguas my mother sorted the coffee and my dad packed it for shipping, which was a big step up from picking the beans. It was a hard life, but what my father wanted was for the kids to be able to go to school. For us, that meant coming to the United States.

"I came to this country when I was seven. I had learned a little English in Caguas, and so I picked it up easy here. One thing I learned was that *señor* in Spanish was *mister* in English. I wanted to be an American boy, so when my cousin called me Señor Morales one time, I told him not to call me Señor. Call me 'Mister.' That was my nickname all the time I was growing up.

"We lived in Brooklyn, and I went to grammar school and junior high in my neighborhood near Macon Street. Then I went to Boys High. Three days after I graduated from high school, I joined the army. The Korean War was on."

"You wanted to fight in the war?" I asked.

"No, what I wanted was for the government to pay for college when I got out. But when I got out, I met Gabriela, that's my wife, and I found myself working at Macy's. But both of us wanted to have our own business one day.

"After our first kid was born, Gabriela worked part-time at this restaurant called Whimpey's. She told me how the guy she worked for spent more time betting on the numbers than he did working the restaurant. When he decided to close the restaurant, she came up with the idea that I should buy it."

"And what did you say?" Cap asked.

"What I said was that I didn't know anything about running a restaurant," Mister M said. "We talked it over, and we agreed to look into it. Meanwhile, I got a part-time job working in the kitchen in Smalls. I'd leave Macy's at five thirty and hotfoot it up to Smalls on 135th Street. I worked at Smalls part-time for almost a year before I was convinced that I could run my own place. Then we bought Whimpey's and called it *Gusto de las Americas*. I worked in it, Gabby worked in it, my brother and two cousins all worked our tails off, and for a long time it was the best small Spanish restaurant in Brooklyn. I just sold it in 1995 because it was time for me to retire and I got a real good offer for it."

"What kind of food you have there?" I asked.

"Everything. You want American food, we had hamburgers, french fries and roast beef. If you want Spanish food, we had *platanos*, *yami*, *tostones* and rice with everything. *Arroz con habichuelas*, *arroz con pollo*, *arroz con* anything you want."

"That sounds pretty good if you want to open a restaurant," Kevin said.

"The trick to the whole thing," Duke said, "is to pick your own road in life. You don't want someone else picking it for you, and you sure don't want to stumble down some road by accident."

"Yeah, it all sounds good," I answered. "But you got a lot of people coming into the barbershop, and you can see that some of them are blowing the set."

"They ran into obstacles," Duke came back. "That's what education, discipline and all that other good stuff I've been talking to you about is for, overcoming the obstacles."

"What you need to do," Kevin said, "is publish a book called *Rules for Every Thing*."

"If I publish a book," Duke said, "I'm going to call it *Handbook for Boys*, maybe even *Handbook for Fast Mouth Boys*."

"And you would do yourself a favor by reading it," Cap said to Kevin. "Give 'em your rules, Duke."

"Rule number one." Duke held one finger in the air. "Figure out what you mean by success. That's a hard one. Sounds easy but it's hard. Because your idea of success might not be my idea. You might want to have a million dollars to spend, and I might just want to have a good job and a little garden. But you got to make that decision somewhere down the line."

"What's the second rule?" I asked. I figured I had the first rule knocked. Figuring out what success was seemed easy.

"The second rule is finding out what work is needed to get to that success," Duke said. "That's where you need to read books, find somebody who has done that thing you want to do, and get all the information you need. That's kind of hard, too. If you want to be an astronaut, you can get an idea what you need to do by reading a book or two, but it's hard to get all the details. That's why so many people in this neighborhood have such a hard time. We don't have enough professionals living in our neighborhoods to serve as role models and to pass down the information that young people need to really pursue success."

"I found out about the work by working in Smalls," Mister M said.

"And the last rule is the easiest," Duke went on. "After you find out what you mean by success, and find out what work is needed to get there, then just go on and do the work. That's rule number three, do the work."

"And I can tell you his restaurant, when he was running it," Cap said, "was every bit as good as he says it was."

"Hey, it was hard work," Mister M said. "But looking back on it, I have to say it was worth it."

"You knew all of Duke's rules?" I asked Mister M.

"Not really," Mister M said. He looked over at Duke and shrugged. "Duke, I'm going to have to tell you the truth. I really didn't know those rules."

"It doesn't make any difference," Duke said. "A lot of people go through life and are successful without knowing all the right rules. A lot of young men enter the family business. Now, they've seen the success of the business and they've decided they want a piece of it."

"And they know the work because they see that, too," I said.

"Will you listen to Jimmy?" Duke said. "He's right. They might not ever sit down and think about rules, but they still follow them."

"Suppose a guy hits the lottery?" Kevin said.

That was so wack, Duke didn't even answer Kevin. I felt like going over and slapping Kevin upside his head, but I didn't.

"Most people don't know Duke's rules of

success," Cap said. "And most people aren't successful. You see the average guy, he's lucky if he gets by from day to day."

"So you're just saying that people like Mister M just kind of lucked into being successful?" I asked.

"No, he thought about it," Duke said. "And he came up with my rules even though he didn't think, 'Hey, I'm doing Duke's rules today.'"

Kevin started talking about how he was going to be an engineer, and Duke cut him off and gave us some boric acid powder to put around in the corners. He said that it kept roaches down. I had a funny feeling about the way he spoke to Kevin, like he was mad at him or something. Duke has a way of letting you know he's mad at you without raising his voice. It was cool.

When Mister M left, I could see he was proud of being successful and of Duke and Cap checking him out. It was something I wanted, too.

"That's quite a man," Duke said. "He's done a lot for this neighborhood. He gives to Little Leagues, block associations, Christmas Fund, everything."

"Can I tell you something?" I said.

"Yeah, go ahead," Duke said.

"I think this is got to be one of those big announcements," Cap said. "Remember that program used to come on Sunday afternoon, and when anybody important talked they had that music that would play?"

"Yeah," Duke said. "Soon as you heard that music, you knew you better stop everything you doing and listen because the good stuff was coming."

"I think I hear the music playing right now," Cap said.

"Later for you guys," I said.

"You want me to hum something?" Kevin asked.

I don't mind when Duke and Cap or Mister M get on my case, but Kevin was getting on my nerves. I gave him a look to let him know I didn't appreciate him running his mouth. Maybe he thought I was scared of him or something.

"What did you have to say?" Duke asked.

"I think your three rules don't work," I said.

"Why is that?" Duke asked.

"Because if it was that simple, everybody would get over," I said.

"That's because you don't understand the three rules," Kevin said.

"I understand them as well as you do," I said.

"No, he understands them all right," Duke said. "And Jimmy's right. Some things are simple to say but they're not simple to do. A lot of people don't even know where to look when they're trying to figure out what success means to them. That's why you hear so many young guys talking about going into the NBA. That's a success they can see, even if they can't play a lick of ball."

"You can be anything you want to be if you set your mind to it," Kevin said.

The old dudes, Duke, Cap and Mister M, were the ones who were supposed to be spitting out weak stuff like that, and there's Kevin, sucking up like some super doofus.

"There's another thing you can do," Duke said, "that's a lot easier and won't give you a headache."

"What?" I asked.

"Just kick back and relax," Duke said. He pulled the handle that let the barber chair go back and crossed his ankles. "Let somebody else sweat getting the good life. You can just teach yourself to get by on whatever comes your way."

On the way home it started raining and I got caught in that. Then I tried to remember Duke's rules, and I could only remember the one about deciding what success meant for you and the one about doing the work. I had forgotten the other one already.

There was a dude I didn't know on the stoop, and he asked me if I could spare two quarters. I thought about all the stuff Duke was talking about, and how maybe people weren't entitled to three meals. I was going to say something wise to the brother but couldn't think of a thing. I gave him a quarter and went on upstairs.

Cap Runs His
Mouth About Reading

Okay, so we ran some ball in the school yard at lunchtime. We were still playing when I heard the bell ring for the afternoon session. I hadn't eaten lunch, so I copped a hot dog from the dude on the corner. It was greasy, but I ate it anyway. Bad news. I went into my first class, which was history, and my stomach was foul. I mean *really* foul.

In history the teacher is Miss Scott, who is not as fly as she thinks she is. She was running down a lot of facts about the civil rights movement from the olden days, but the big thing she was trying to knock everybody out with was that her moms was down in Alabama and whatnot marching and carrying on. The class was hip even though I had heard most of the stuff before, and my stomach was not correct, so halfway through the class I raised my hand and asked for the pass to go to the bathroom.

Miss Scott got an attitude like I had dissed her mother or something.

"The civil rights movement represents sacrifices by a lot of people for every American, white or black," she said.

She was of the white persuasion, so I guess that meant that I was supposed to sit there and look stupid and happy while she ran the whole thing down. I had to go to the bathroom, so I got up and left.

The thing ended up with me going to the principal's office and explaining to him that my stomach was upset. Then I had to listen to him mouth off about the civil rights movement. Mr. Harris is black. He rambled on about what I needed to do and how I needed to do it, just like every other adult in my life.

So all that is what I was dragging into the barbershop.

It was just a little past three when I got there. The old guys were talking about how they hated cell phones.

"It used to be," Duke was saying, "that if you saw a fellow standing on the corner and talking in a loud voice and you didn't see anybody else there, you could be pretty sure the guy was crazy as a loon and it was time for you to cross the street."

"That's sure the truth," Cap said.

"Now you're liable to see a cell phone in his hand," Duke said. "And you don't know if there's anybody on the other end of that phone or not."

I was dusting the stupid plants as usual when Duke asked me what was on my mind. I should have said nothing, but instead I told him that when the civil rights thing was happening, it was easier to deal with your life than it is now.

"If people are making their dogs bite you and bombing your church, or putting up signs about how you can't drink out of their fountains and stuff, then you know what you got to do," I said. "If none of that is going on, then you just kind of slide and see what's what."

"You mean to tell me," Duke said, speaking slow, "that you can see half the young men on this street without jobs, more people than you

85

want to know from this block ending up in jail, and you still need a bomb and a sign to tell you what to do?"

"Hey, I'm just trying to keep it real," I said.

Before Duke answered, Kevin came in, late as usual, carrying a cage. He put it on the floor in the corner. In the corner of the cage there was a little furry thing.

"Hamster," Kevin said. "I have to feed him fresh vegetables and grains for a month. Another kid has one, and he's going to feed his junk food. Then we'll check them out to see which is the healthiest."

"I bet the hamster with the junk food is going to be the healthiest," Mister M said. "Animals are supposed to be fat. They're different than humans."

Duke told Kevin to get a paint scraper and go over the floor looking for gum.

"Scrape it up good," Duke said. "There's nothing nastier than a floor that's covered with old gum." Kevin gave me a look and shook his head. We both knew there wouldn't be much gum, if any, stuck on any floor that Duke owned, but it didn't mean Kevin didn't have to get the scraper and start looking.

"Jimmy, get yourself a hammer and a nail

and put this sign up," Cap said.

"There's a hammer in the closet over there under the picture of Martin Luther King, Jr.," Duke said.

I went over to the narrow closet that Duke keeps tools and cleaning stuff in and got the hammer.

"And don't break my sign, boy," Cap said, handing me a package wrapped in brown paper.

"You want me to open it up?" I asked.

"No, put it on the wall all wrapped up so nobody can read it," Cap said. "Now what kind of sense does that make?"

"I just asked, man," I said. "You don't have to bite my head off."

"Will you listen to Jimmy?" Mister M said, jerking his thumb toward me. "He's not old enough for his pee to get a real stink to it and he's got the nerve to catch an attitude."

I started taking the paper off of Cap's sign just as a customer came in. He was tall and Spanishy-looking and needed a haircut bad.

"Manuel!" Duke grabbed the customer's hand and shook it. "I heard you started your own business up in the Bronx?"

"Nothing big," Manuel said, settling into

the barber's chair. "I'm selling a little furniture. You know anybody needs a good bedroom set, or a living-room set, let me know."

"You got good stuff?" Mister M asked.

"It's not the *real* good stuff," Manuel said, checking himself out in the mirror, "but it's okay if you don't have any big money."

"I know what you mean," Mister M said. "You have to crawl before you can walk."

"Don't take too much off the top," Manuel said. Duke was putting that little paper thing around his neck. "But make me look conservative."

"I'll make you look like a banker," Duke said.

I put a nail in the wooden panel between the mirrors and hung Cap's sign right in the middle.

"Put it up a little higher," Cap said. "About level with the calendar."

"Why didn't you tell me to do that in the first place?" I asked.

"Boy, your mouth is running faster than it can drag your butt behind it," Mister M said.

I let that slide, but they were working big-time on my nerves, and I think they knew it, too.

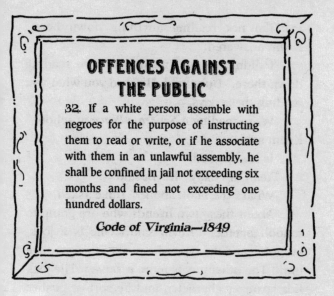

OFFENCES AGAINST THE PUBLIC

32. If a white person assemble with negroes for the purpose of instructing them to read or write, or if he associate with them in an unlawful assembly, he shall be confined in jail not exceeding six months and fined not exceeding one hundred dollars.

Code of Virginia—1849

"Jimmy, can you dance?" Duke asked, when I had put the hammer back.

"Yeah."

"Good," Duke said. "Let's see you grab that broom and dance around the floor with it a couple of times."

That was so corny it wasn't even funny, but that's the kind of stuff I had to hear every day in the barbershop.

"Hey, bright eyes, what you reading these days?" Duke called down to Kevin.

"I'm not reading anything down here," Kevin answered.

"I didn't ask you what you were reading down there," Duke said. "I asked you what you reading these days."

"We're reading *A Separate Peace* in school," Kevin said.

"Is it any good?"

"Yeah, it's okay," Kevin said.

"What's the book about?" Duke asked.

"About these two friends who are going to school together," Kevin said. "One is a jock, outgoing and the type who pushes things to the limit. The other guy is more reserved. The jock is a stronger character, and he sort of pushes the other guy around. I haven't finished it yet, so I don't know how it turns out."

"Jimmy, what are you reading?" Duke asked.

"You want the truth?" I answered.

"No," Cap said, "he wants a salami sandwich on rye bread."

"I'm not reading anything right now," I said. "'Cause everything they want us to read in school is boring."

"Well, that's good," Cap said. "I like to see a young man that doesn't read."

90

"Why is that, Cap?" Mister M asked.

Cap lowered his voice a little and put his hand over his mouth like I wasn't supposed to hear him. "I'll tell you when Jimmy's not around," he said.

"Yo, Cap, you know you can't stop running your mouth, man," I said. "So why don't you go on and say what you got to say."

"We need people who don't read," Cap said. "Let's say Manuel here expands his business until he's doing several million dollars a year."

"Sounds good to me," Manuel said from the chair.

"And let's say a huge company calls him and wants to know if he can supply them with six thousand couches by the end of the month," Cap went on. "Manuel thinks about it for a minute and then realizes he wants a cup of coffee. Right away he's going to look around for somebody to run out and get him some coffee. Now, he can't send somebody out who's a good reader because he needs his readers to run his business. So when he spots a young man who doesn't read, his problem is solved."

"I didn't say I couldn't read," I said. "I said I'm not reading anything right now."

"Hey, Cap, I think you got it wrong," Duke

said. "Jimmy is going to drop out of high school, go straight into the NBA and make about nineteen million dollars a year like the last five thousand young boys who came through that door. Isn't that right, Jimmy?"

"Whatever." I wasn't going where he wanted me to go.

"Another good reason people shouldn't read," Cap said, "is that most of the time they won't even know what they're missing from life. That's why, way back in slavery times, it was illegal to teach the Negroes, as we were called then, to read. The owners didn't want them reading and figuring out how to get on with their lives and maybe running away from the plantations. So if the boss needs somebody to go fetch some coffee, or carry some bags to a car, he got a whole new crop of people who don't read and won't mind doing it."

"You're coming down hard, Cap," Kevin said.

"I'm not coming down hard, Kevin," Cap said. He crossed one big leg over the other and pulled on his ankle. "There's a fellow downtown who said all of this country is going to be divided into two groups. One group is going to run the country and lead the Good Life. The

92

other group is going to be the Flunky Group. Now what he proposes is for the Good Life Group to build a bunch of prison camps to keep the Flunky Group in, so when they get mad about having to scrape by on handouts from the Good Life Group and start acting up, we'll have someplace to put them. But the way I figure, if we just keep them away from books, they won't mind so much."

"They're really going to do that?" Manuel asked.

"I think they've already started it," Cap said. "You see how many prisons they're building? And you might have noticed they're not going to the colleges looking for recruits. Too much reading going on in the colleges."

"That's true," Manuel said. "You know, I never thought of that. But how come there aren't any protests? You would think that if somebody put you in the group that wasn't doing anything, you would get mad."

"I guess it beats getting bored," Cap said. "Ain't that the truth, Jimmy?"

"I'm not in this conversation anymore," I said.

Duke finished cutting Manuel's hair, and he got out of the chair and checked himself out in

the mirror. He and Duke rapped a bit more about his furniture business, and Duke told him he could put a small sign in the window advertising his business if it was printed neatly. Manuel paid for his haircut and was smiling when he left.

"Did you read that sign I asked you to put up?" Cap went on. "About how it was illegal during slavery times to teach a Negro to read?"

"Yeah, I read it," I said.

"If they bring slavery back," Kevin said, "Jimmy's going to fit right in. They won't even have to teach him nothing."

"If I punch you in your face, maybe you'll fit right in, too," I said. "How about that?"

"Hey, Jimmy, lighten up, man," Mister M said. "You don't want to talk about hitting your friends."

"Yeah, I understand it."

"Can you imagine that?" Cap still couldn't keep his mouth shut. "Here we are, trying to keep him from being a slave for the rest of his life, and he's mad."

"My life is my problem," I said. "I'll worry about my own problems. I don't need none of you to worry about me. Okay?"

"I'm not worried about you," Cap said.

"But if you got something new going on, I want in on it before the rest of the world finds out about it. I mean, here we got a young man who doesn't read because it's boring, so you figure he's got something new that's going to get him over. Maybe I can invest in it and make a few dollars. What's your secret weapon?"

"Just get off my back, man!" I said.

"You know, I had a dog that didn't read," Mister M said. "But he had a heck of a bite. How you bite?"

I threw the broom down and left. Later for all of them.

All the way home all I could think about was knocking all of them out. One by one.

When Moms came home, I tried to get it together, but she peeped the whole show.

"What are you upset about?" she asked.

"I'm tired of people on my back," I said. "I'm just tired of it, that's all."

Tools

Duke came to the house. When I got home, he was sitting in the living room having coffee with Moms. As soon as I saw him, my stomach tightened up and I wondered if he had come to say that I had to go to the juvenile facility. The drapes were closed, and the dark room made the whole scene seem heavy. I wished I had told Moms I hadn't been to the barbershop for the past three days.

"Jimmy?" Mom's voice sounded small.

I sat down on the end of the couch and took a deep breath.

"I just dropped by to see what you were going to do," Duke said.

I searched for some words, but none came. Moms began to talk to me; her voice seemed so weak and sad.

"Jimmy, don't throw away this chance," Moms said. "Please, baby."

"All they do is put me down every day," I said. "I don't know what's worse. Being locked up or this stuff."

"Yeah, you know what's worse," Duke said. "You're not stupid. You don't want to be locked up, because you know where that road leads. I know where it leads, and you know Cap worked in that system for years and he knows where it leads.

"Now, if you want, you can choose to go into some warehouse for young people, get yourself a record and learn a lot about how to commit new crimes," he went on. "And that's about all you'll learn if you're locked up. Of course, when you get out, you can stand on the corner and tell people that you just got out of jail and we both know there's some knuckle-head that's going to be impressed by it. If that's what you want, then just let me know and

I'll report it to the judge."

"Can he have another chance?" Moms asked.

"He's the one sitting here trying to make up his mind," Duke said. "He's thinking about how good jail is going to feel."

"Jimmy?" Moms's voice cracked a little.

"I want another chance," I said.

"I'm going to tell you this one time," Duke said, "so listen carefully. Me and Cap and Mister M have seen a thousand young men like you come through this neighborhood, come through the doors of my barbershop. Too many of them end up lying on some sidewalk with a chalk mark around their bodies. Too many of them end up in jail. Too many of them end up pushing a broom around some factory at night when they should have been running a business or practicing some profession. The big thing with most of these young men is that there are things they just don't understand, and what we're trying to do is to teach you some of these things down at the shop."

"But Cap's saying things like I should read, and no matter what I say, he's acting like I'm wrong," I said.

99

"It's not that you're wrong, Jimmy, it's that your approach needs a lot of work. To me, just being alive in America is like having a box of tools that I can use to build any kind of life I want," Duke said. "But I have to use those tools and build my own life. No one is going to do it for me. Too many young people think that because somebody down the road has said you deserve this or deserve that, then all you have to do is wait around until it comes your way. Believe me, it won't. And it doesn't make any difference if you're a good person or a bad person. Reading is just one of those tools you need to use."

"Yeah, I guess you're right."

"When you came into the shop the other day and started talking to us about the civil rights movement, you stirred up a lot of memories and I was hard on you," Duke said. "I was hard on you, but when I thought about it later, I realized you were right about some of the things you were saying. I'm sorry I didn't see that at the time. My life was a lot easier than yours in a lot of ways. I didn't have the opportunities that you have, and we fought for those opportunities during the movement. But I didn't have the chances to throw my life away the way young people have today. I didn't need to know all of the things you need to look out for these days. But there are too many young people out here needing help for us to throw it away on you if you don't want it."

"I want it," I said.

"I hope so," Duke said, standing up. "I'll expect you down at the shop tomorrow."

When Duke left, Moms was so nervous she was shaking. We went out for Chinese food and brought it home. I knew she wanted to talk to me, and she started a few times, but she didn't know what to say. Finally she just took my hands in hers and held them against her cheek. She was crying, and I felt terrible. But I was glad I was going back.

Duke saying he was sorry was really heavy. He was okay, and I knew he was okay. I just had to figure out how to deal with it.

One Hundred Forty-fifth Street used to be clean, but now it's getting to be dirty all the time. The city doesn't pick up the garbage every day, and sometimes there's garbage piled up and the little kids play on it. The garbage on the sidewalks down near the corner fit my mood perfectly as I walked to the barbershop.

"Hey, I thought you were on a worldwide

tour!" Mister M said in his high voice.

I didn't say anything. I was surprised to see the broom lying in the middle of the floor, just where I had thrown it. The floor was really dirty—there was hair everywhere, and I knew they had left it for me to sweep up. I picked up the broom and started in. Kevin was washing the mirror, and I wondered if they had talked to him about me. I hoped not.

"Duke, do you remember when the Harlem Rens used to play basketball over at the armory?" Mister M asked, ignoring me. "That was when nobody dunked and they used to have that thing when they would go into a weave and run plays off that. You remember the weave?"

"Sure I remember the weave. I remember the Rens, too, because I played against them once," Duke answered. "I wasn't on a regular team, but I played with the Jersey City Whirlwinds when they came over for an exhibition game. The Whirlwinds only brought five men with them, so they picked up two guys who came to see the game."

"How come they only brought five men?" Mister M asked.

"I think because the Rens wiped them up when they played them in Jersey City," Duke said. "When they came—"

Duke stopped in the middle of a sentence and was looking through the front window. We all turned to see what he was looking at. Out on the street there was a woman standing in the middle of the sidewalk. Some small kids were looking at her. It didn't take a whole lot of looking to see she was a junkie. She had medium-brown skin and dark eyes. She had a nice smile, but her teeth were a little ratty looking.

"Why on earth do people have to use that stuff?" Cap asked.

"Yo, I know why they use drugs," Kevin said.

"Should have known one of you two guys was responsible," Cap said.

"Go outside and ask that girl where she was raised, Jimmy," Duke said. "I think I've seen her around here before."

"I don't want to talk to no junkie," I said.

"Go ahead, Kevin." Duke pointed at Kevin and then pointed at the woman doing her junkie nod on the sidewalk.

"I can't just go out and start asking her

questions," Kevin said.

Duke told Mister M to go ask her if she wanted her hair touched up. Mister M did, and she came into the barbershop with him.

"How you doing, sister?" Duke sat her up in the chair and put an apron over her.

"Fine, Mr. Duke," the woman answered. "You know my mother used to live in the same building you did over on Seventh Avenue."

"Irene Davis," Duke said. "I thought I recognized you. How is your mother?"

"She's doing pretty good," Irene said. "Got a touch of arthritis and can't get around as much as she used to."

"Sorry to hear that," Duke said. "Tell her I said hello. She's a sweet woman. You want me to trim around the edges for you?"

"That's a good way of getting new business," Irene said.

"So how are you doing today?" Duke asked as he began to trim her hair around the edges.

"I'm making it," she said. "You know it's hard out there these days."

Duke trimmed Irene's hair and talked to her. Every once in a while she would nod out a little, and then Duke would speak a little louder and she would sit up again. She said she had lived in the neighborhood most of her life.

"Except for about two years when I had me a room down on 120th Street across from the park," she said.

"Garvey Park?" Cap asked.

"No, Morningside Park," she said. She was scratching the back of her hand as she talked.

Just then this big, dark, cornbread-looking brother came in. Duke and Cap both nodded toward him. He was about six feet six, maybe even taller. He sat down and put the briefcase he was carrying under his chair. I thought he might be Kevin's parole officer or something.

Duke finished trimming Irene's hair and sprayed it with some hair oil. She looked a lot better than she did when she came in. When she left, I thought she had a little bounce in her walk, too.

"Dr. Ernie Colfax, my main man." Duke went over to the big guy who had come in and shook his hand.

"How you doing, Duke?" The guy stood when he shook hands, and he looked like a giant next to Duke.

"Ernie here was raised right on 149th

Street," Cap said. "Played basketball in college and could have had a long career in the NBA if he wanted. Decided to become a doctor instead."

"You could have been in the NBA?" I asked.

"I sat on the bench in Phoenix for two years, and then I sat on the bench in Milwaukee for two more," Dr. Colfax said. "I wanted to go to medical school and decided to get on with my life. Am I next?"

"Yeah, sit yourself down," Duke said. "You see that young lady who was just in here?"

"Saw the scabs on her veins," Dr. Colfax said.

"Why do these people use drugs, Ernie?" Duke asked. "Are they really that exciting?"

"There are a number of theories," Dr. Colfax said. "Most black physicians think it starts with frustration for some, and experimentation for others. But the name of the game is addiction. Some people have what we call addictive personalities, and just a little 'try it out' can mean a lifetime of pain."

"It's messed up being a head," I said. "Your whole thing gets to be raggedy. Can't keep no job, got to steal or sell your body to get straight. Your whole life is twisted around a needle or crack or whatever you're messing with."

"There's AIDS out there, too," Cap said. "If they don't kill each other looking to rob some drugs, they're liable to end up with AIDS. And the big A will definitely take you on out of this world."

"Ernie, you're a doctor. Do you think Irene was feeling good nodding out there in the middle of the sidewalk?" Duke asked.

"Not really, but she's got her life down to such a low level that if she didn't get her drugs, she'd feel sick and even more depressed than she normally feels," Dr. Colfax said. "So in a way she's feeling better for a short time until the drugs wear off, then she starts feeling sick again and looking for more drugs."

"And what made her start using drugs in the first place?" Cap asked. "She said she's lived in this neighborhood most of her life. You mean to tell me she's seen other junkies in the street and said, 'Boy, that sure looks like a good life?'"

"People hear about it and want to try it out," I said.

"What have you heard about drugs that's good," Duke asked, "that would make you want to experiment with them?"

"People get trapped in a particular situation," Dr. Colfax said, "and they don't know how to get out of the situation. They get desperate and do things that don't even make sense to them as they do it."

"I think they're just stupid," Cap said. "All the bad stuff they got in the papers about crack and heroin, and these young people running down the street trying to get it. To me it's like jumping off a tall building without a parachute because you feel so good coming down."

"And suppose their friends give them some drugs for free," Kevin interrupted. "Then maybe they want to be strong, but the urge gets to be too much and they get messed up again."

"Then they need to find themselves some new friends," Duke said.

When Dr. Colfax's haircut was finished, he asked me and Kevin if we played ball, and we both said we did. I didn't even say anything about Kevin not having a game. The old guys got into some other ball players they knew and who had a good game and who didn't. I dug the conversation because the brother was a doctor and a ball player and that was together. I asked him was it hard becoming a doctor.

"Sure it was," he said. "But hard doesn't mean bad, does it?"

"Depends on how hard," I said.

The end of the day came, and I hung until everybody had left and then I thanked Duke for giving me another chance.

"You're the next generation," Duke said. "Young people like you and Kevin have to get ready to run the world. Whatever future I got you're going to be a part of it, one way or another. If what I believe in makes a difference, then your generation is going to have to prove it. Did you learn anything today?"

"Not to use drugs," I said.

"No, Jimmy, that wasn't it." Duke pulled the gate across the window of the barbershop. "You knew that before you came in today. So did Irene before she started using that stuff. What you should have learned is that just because we know something is liable to ruin our lives, it doesn't mean we're not going to do it. We have to pay close attention to what we're doing every day."

"It makes you mad to see somebody like Irene, doesn't it?"

"It breaks my heart," Duke said. "It really does."

When I got home, I told Moms what had happened in the shop and what Dr. Colfax had said about drugs. I said I wasn't ever going to use drugs.

"Everybody says that," Moms said.

"Yeah, but I mean it," I said.

"I hope so, Jimmy," she said. She kissed me. "I hope so."

When I went to bed, I thought about Irene. The neighborhood wasn't just about crack heads, but I had seen enough of them to know what being a junkie was all about. On television they just showed guys selling rock on the corner and maybe running from the cops. They never showed guys all bent over and sick and looking up at you with sick eyes. They never showed you a girl like Irene begging for money or going with some guy into a dark hall to do whatever she had to do to get the money for crack.

What Duke said about doing things that

could ruin your life didn't make a whole lot of sense to me. On the other hand, I saw people doing it every day. Maybe he was right—life didn't work. At least not the way I thought it should.

Taking Care of the Ball

On Sunday morning Moms was trying to get me to go to church with her. She wanted to go to a different church than the one she usually went to on 141st Street, and I was thinking about going when the telephone rang. Sometimes Uncle Gilbert went to church with Moms, and I hoped it wasn't him. I had taken Bailey to the park Saturday morning and tried to teach her a trick and a whole bunch of little kids gathered around, saw what I was doing and said that my dog was stupid. I didn't want anything more to do with Bailey or Uncle Gilbert. I was listening to Moms on the phone and I heard her saying, "Yes, Mr. Wilson," and I knew it was Duke.

"I'm sure he's going to be thrilled, Mr. Wilson," Moms was saying as she came into the kitchen with the cordless phone. Then, without putting her hand over the telephone so I could say anything without it being heard, she told me that Duke had tickets to the Knicks game that afternoon and how she knew I wanted to go.

"Yes, he does!" Moms said as I shook my head no. "Okay, he'll meet you in front of the shop at two fifteen. We'll be out of church by then. All right. I know you guys will have a wonderful time."

"Moms, what did you get me into?" I asked when she had hung up the phone.

What she had got me into was going to a Knicks game with Duke that afternoon. It was, like, really embarrassing. You see all these guys on television taking kids to the park and buying them ice cream and then this message comes on about "Be a friend to a child in need," and now Duke was taking me to a ball game. I tried to explain to Moms that the whole scene was super lame.

"It's not like anybody's wrong or anything,"

I said, "but I ain't no little kid and I sure ain't no orphan."

Moms has a bag of tricks she uses on me. This time she reached into it and pulled out the one about "Will you do it just this one time for me?" I said no, and she tried it again, this time with a little quiver in her voice and biting her lip like she was fixing to cry.

Okay, so I met Duke in front of the shop, and we stood around and talked for almost a half hour and I was thinking that maybe he really didn't have the tickets. Then he went to the corner and made a phone call. When he got off the phone, he came back to me and said that Kevin couldn't make it. So now I figured that Kevin felt the same way I did but he had the guts to get out of it, and I felt really stupid.

"You go to a lot of games?" I asked as the A train rocked its way down toward 34th Street and Madison Square Garden.

"I used to go with my wife," Duke said. "Back in the seventies we used to get season tickets. When they got so expensive, we would still go once in a while, but not as much as we did in the seventies."

"She was down with basketball?"

"She liked the game a lot," Duke said.

114

"When our son played in the Biddy league, she went to the library and read up on the game."

Duke's son was in the Air Force and lived in California. I asked Duke if his son was still playing ball.

"No. He's a chaplain in the service, and he's pretty busy."

"A chaplain?" I realized right away I had said it too loud.

"You don't like chaplains?" Duke asked.

"You have a real good son, and now you're dealing with me and Kevin," I said. "That's got to be different, right?"

"Meaning that my boy is good and you and Kevin are bad?" Duke asked.

"Something like that."

We got off at 34th Street and walked over toward the Garden. It was a warm Sunday afternoon, and the streets were jammed with people. In front of the Garden there were guys hustling tickets and people selling pennants and little orange basketballs. We had forty minutes to kill before the game started, so we went downstairs under the Garden to one of the restaurants. Duke ordered an orange drink and a hot dog, and I just had an iced tea.

"There are bad people in the world," Duke

said. "Some old bad people and some young bad people, and I'm not interested in being around any of them. Most young people who get into trouble aren't bad. They just don't realize that there are things in their lives that need to be taken care of, need to be nurtured. You were talking to Cap about reading the other day. Reading is something you need to take care of in your life. You don't take care of it and you're going to have a hard way to go. Having a plan to succeed is something you need to tend to as well. You ever see an old man with a bicycle around the neighborhood? Got a little basket on the handlebars?"

"Sometimes he's got a cat in that basket?"

"Yeah, that's him. Man's had that bicycle for as long as I can remember," Duke said. "He takes care of that bicycle, and it gets him around the neighborhood. You see some youngsters with brand-new bicycles and they break them up, lose them and just don't take care of them."

"So life is like a bicycle, right?"

"You're grinning," Duke said, "so you got to think I'm talking some old-timey stuff."

"I didn't say that," I said.

"Yeah, it's old-timey," Duke said. "But let

me ask you this. When Cap asked you about you taking care of your reading, was he the only one who knew how important reading was, or did you know it, too? Don't be too quick to answer, now. You're not on television and I'm not giving you a million dollars if you get the right answer."

"Can I call my Moms as my expert friend?"

"Yeah, go on."

We went upstairs to the Garden, and the crowd was huge. Duke went to the ticket window and left Kevin's ticket just in case he changed his mind.

By the time we got to our seats, I was getting excited about being at the game. The crowd was going and the organ player was doing his thing. We had good seats, and Duke read the program as I watched the players on the court warm up. It was a nice time, and I didn't feel so self-conscious about being at the game with Duke.

Okay, so the Knicks were playing Miami and the set got physical from the jump. We were close enough to hear the players' sneakers squeak on the floor and hear them shouting back and forth.

"If they announced on the loudspeaker that

the Knicks needed one more player and any-body that could play please come down to the court, would you go?" Duke asked, during a time-out.

"I'd give it a try," I said.

"You know what your first problem would be?"

"What?"

"Not to get trampled by all the other guys running down to the court," Duke said.

At the end of the first half the Heat were

ahead by three points. The Knicks made a comeback in the second half, and then the Heat got ahead again with two minutes to go. I thought the Knicks were going to lose, but then Mourning fouled out and Sprewell made two quick baskets to tie the game with thirty seconds to go. I figured overtime. But the guard for the Heat brought the ball up, made a quick move around a pick and got called for traveling.

"That was stupid," I said.

The Knicks had the ball with seven seconds and called a time-out. I thought they were going to give it to Sprewell. The Heat closed Sprewell off, and the ball came into Camby and he got fouled at the buzzer. Then he missed the first shot.

"If he misses the second shot, I'm asking for my money back," Duke said.

He made the second shot, the Knicks won and me, Duke and the crowd left the Garden happy.

"I knew about reading being important," I said to Duke as we walked over toward the east side train. "I can really read well when I want to."

"I could be wrong, but I think sometimes

we think we know something, and we don't know as much about it as we should," Duke said. "How do we know when we know something? See that guy over there in the blue jacket?"

I looked over and saw this dude with a stomach sticking out so far he looked like he was pregnant. He was eating some french fries from a bag.

"Do you think he knows he's fat enough to cut his life short?" Duke asked.

"Yeah, he knows it," I said. "But sometimes, you know, just because you know something doesn't mean you're going to do it."

"So you think if you walked over to that brother and said, 'Hey, you know you're going to die about ten years too soon,' he'd put the french fries down?" Duke said. "Or do you think he'll say, 'Maybe I won't die and maybe I'll do something about it tomorrow'?"

"That's what he's going to say," I answered. "But in a way he knows it and in a way he doesn't know it. And I'm not going to go over there and ask him, so don't tell me to."

"Now you have the whole thing in a nutshell," Duke said. "I thought it was going to take three or four years, but you got it locked up. Now you can sit over on the side with me and Cap and tell the young boys what to do."

I looked over at Duke and expected to see him smiling, but he wasn't. He started talking about basketball, how the players of today were so much faster and stronger than in his day.

"But the tickets were a lot cheaper," he said.

We got to 145th Street quickly and he told me he was thinking about getting some old photographs of the neighborhood from the library and putting them up in the barbershop to decorate the place. I liked the idea and said I'd go to the library with him if he wanted.

"So, did going to the game with Duke destroy you?" Moms asked when I got in the house.

"No, it was good," I said.

Kevin called about eight o'clock and said that Duke had asked him if he wanted to go.

"I told him I'd go," Kevin said. "But there was no way I was going to go for that 'I'm your substitute daddy' thing."

"He bought the tickets," I said.

"That's on him," Kevin said. "You went for it?"

"Yeah," I said. "And I dug it."

"Did he hold your hand when you crossed the streets?"

"Why don't you ask me that tomorrow when you see me in the shop?" I said, and hung up.

I hadn't dug Duke's taking me to the game too tough at first either, but I saw he was just trying to be in my corner and helping me to get my stuff correct. You don't goof on somebody like that.

The thing was, when I went to bed, I was thinking about my dad, and about what Moms said about him. The more I thought about him, I was thinking that maybe he wasn't a foul dude or anything like that, but he definitely wasn't taking care of business as far as I was concerned. And the way Duke and Cap was running it, maybe he didn't even realize he wasn't taking care of business. That was heavy, but I could see it being real.

S-E-X

I hit the shop one minute late, but nobody noticed because the place was jammed. Duke was there, Mister M, Cap, Mack from down the street, Kevin and this fellow named Tariq Brewer. Tariq's twenty, can sing a little and thinks he's a killer MC but his rap is tired. I didn't even have to hear what he was saying to know that Duke and Cap didn't go for it. You could just see it by the way they kind of leaned back and narrowed their eyes. That's the thing about old dudes—you could just look at them sometimes and know what they were thinking.

"Women just naturally love me because I

treat them right," Tariq was saying. "I give them that deep feeling that they all want."

"How many children you say you got out there?" Mister M asked.

"I got three shorties," Tariq said. "And you know I'm right there for them. Just the way I love women, that's the same way I love my kids."

"You married to any of the mamas?" Mister M asked.

"I got too much nature for one woman," Tariq answered, smiling. "Some men are just like that. God gave me the gift of being a lover."

"And who's supporting your babies?" Mister M asked. "I heard you weren't working."

"Hey, I'm not asking you who's supporting your woman," Tariq said. "They're getting by good. I check them out all the time, make sure they got what they need. You're a man just like me. You got to do what you got to do and I got to do what I got to do. Case closed."

"You're not afraid of catching something with all these diseases going around?" Mister M asked.

"I don't mess with no funky women," Tariq said. "If they don't keep themselves clean and nice, I don't even talk to them. If you see some

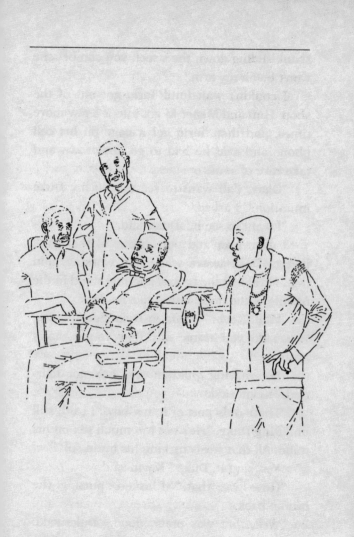

skank sliding down the street, you can bet she won't be on my arm."

I couldn't wait until Tariq got out of the shop. Him and Mister M got into it a few more times, and then Tariq got a page on his cell phone and said he had to go downtown and take care of some business.

"Okay, y'all want to see me do my Duke imitation?" I asked.

"I want to see it," Duke said.

I went over and put on one of the white jackets Duke wears when he's working, and then I grabbed the broom and just stood in the middle of the floor with it like he does.

"Well, Kevin," I said in Duke's deep voice, "what do you think was that young man's problem?"

"He's having children and he's not married," Kevin said.

"That's only part of it, my boy," I said, still imitating Duke. "He's got too much sex on his mind. All that sex is turning his brain soft."

"Yes, sir, Mr. Duke," Kevin said.

"How was that?" I asked, putting the broom back.

"Well, that was pretty good," Duke said. "But Tariq's problem goes a little further than that. He's one of these young men who believe that if he's not thinking about something, it's not happening. So if he's not thinking about it when the kids need him, he can fool himself into thinking they don't need him. If he's not thinking about their mamas needing him, then he can tell himself they're probably all right."

"See no evil, hear no evil and speak no evil," Cap said. "People like him run through life leaving a whole string of little mini disasters in their wake."

"Then if he wakes up one morning and finds he has AIDS or some venereal disease, he's going to think the world has done him wrong," Duke went on.

"So we got to add 'Don't have sex' to your list of rules?" Kevin asked.

"You don't have to add anything about sex to my rules," Duke said. "I know what I'm about. I know I don't want to bring children into the world that I'm not willing to take care of and support. And I'm not ready to risk my health for a few minutes of pleasure. Now, that's me. What you want to do with your life is your business."

"He said he wasn't going out with any funky women," Kevin said.

"You get **AIDS** from people because they're *funky?*" Cap asked.

"No, I know you get it from blood or other body liquids," Kevin came back. "But at least it helps if they're not dirty-looking."

"Dirty doesn't have a thing to do with AIDS," Cap said. "You can go down to the City Hospital and see some of the cleanest people in the world sitting around trying to hold on to life a little longer because they have AIDS. Mack can tell you that. He worked in the hospital for a while. Isn't that right, Mack?"

"Yeah, but I don't know if you can just give up sex altogether," Mack said. "Everybody gets them urges for pleasure, man. And women know that, too. That's why they dress so sexy."

"There's nothing wrong with pleasure," Duke said. "But let me ask you this. When we talk about pleasure, and having a good time, does that mean I have to open the door to the barbershop and put my character outside until we finish grinning and winking about how good some woman looks?"

"Hey, I didn't say that," Mack said. "But when a man gets excited, you can never tell what he's going to do. He might have to yield to temptation if the girl looks good enough. You know, I'm a single man, and when I see a pretty woman, my eye lingers and I just kind of start itching all over."

"Sex is an instinct," Kevin said. "It's not something that you sit down and figure out a checklist of should-I's and shouldn't-I's. I mean, if you're thinking of robbing a bank, you have to figure out your chances of getting caught or getting shot or something like that. But sex is different."

"You don't have to worry about a thing," Cap said. "Just close your eyes and let the good times roll. Ain't that right?"

"Look, I don't mean any disrespect," Kevin said. I could tell he thought he was cooking. "But you and Duke are old. Sex is different for you when you get old. A young man thinks different."

"I think he's got something there," Duke said. "Tariq thinks that having three children out here in the world makes him a real man. I guess that's a young man's idea. You lie down with a woman and you stand up a man."

"Unless you're using protection," Kevin said. "Then you don't have to worry about no shorties showing up, or disease."

"I know that's not right," I said. "Everybody knows about birth control and whatnot, and every year there are girls dropping out of school and having kids. And that's only at our school."

"Well, you do what you do as a man," Kevin said, "and I'll do what I do."

"Duke, can I ask you a personal question?" I asked.

"You can ask, but it doesn't mean I'm going to answer you," Duke said.

"When you were young and single," I asked, "didn't you want to fool around sometimes?"

Duke thought for a minute, then picked up his paper. At first I thought he wasn't going to answer me, but he did. "Yeah, sure I did," he said. "I know you're going to find this hard to believe, but girls were just as exciting when I was young as they are today. And there have always been some girls you could talk into going a little further than they should. Things weren't much different for me than they are for you. But look around your neighborhood. Ask yourself what's going to happen to all of these children being born to young

mothers who aren't more than children themselves. Then ask yourself what you have to do
with the whole scene."

Of all the things Duke and the old-timers
said, the stuff about sex was the hardest to deal
with. Mostly because when you were thinking
about doing it, you weren't thinking about
shorties and AIDS and all that kind of stuff. It
was like everything they were saying was right,
but there wasn't a real connection between
doing the nasty and what came later.

When I got home, I thought about running
it down to Moms, but I knew what she was
going to say. It was one of those things that
everybody knew but, like Duke said, maybe
you didn't want to keep on your mind.

Lonnie G

I saw Kevin at the 145th Street station. He was talking to three friends of his, and they turned and looked at me. He waved me over and I went and said hello.

"Jimmy works in the barbershop with me," Kevin told them.

"Kevin said you get a sermon every day," said one of Kevin's friends. He was a big, heavy dude wearing a T-shirt and a tie. That was supposed to be hip.

"Yeah, something like that," I said.

We came out of the subway and Kevin's

friends headed up Edgecombe, and me and Kevin started down the hill toward the barber-shop.

"All those guys are going to go to college," Kevin said. "They're probably the smartest students in the school."

"That's important to you, huh?"

"You got to hang with the best if you want to learn what the best are doing," Kevin said. "That's why you're lucky to be hanging with me."

"I ain't hanging with you," I said. "I'm stuck with you."

We got to the barbershop, and a thin, gray-haired woman was standing in the doorway. She had light-brown skin and nervous hands, which she kept wiping on her apron. As I slid past her into the barbershop, I saw that her eyes were red.

"Pray for me, Brother Mills," the woman said.

"You know you have my prayers, Sister Davis," Cap said.

The woman looked down and shook her head. "I can't believe my heart has to be broken like this," she said. "My soul is weary to bear this burden alone!"

"We're all going to pray for you, and for the boy," Cap said.

The woman was crying when she left. I watched her go down the street. She looked big and round, and her steps were slow and heavy, as if she could hardly lift her feet to walk. Earl, from the curio shop, was playing checkers against Cap.

"What happened to her?" Kevin asked.

"That's Lonnie G's grandmother," Duke said. "Lonnie G tried to hold up the supermarket across the street. He pulled a gun on the manager, got the money and then tried to escape out the back door. That back door leads to a blind alley. He ran out there, and the manager closed the door and locked it behind him. All they had to do then was to wait for the cops to come and pick up his sorry butt."

"Lonnie G did that?" I asked. "I know he's got an attitude, but I didn't think he would pull a stickup."

"His grandmother said he was trying to get some money so he could get married," Earl said. "I guess he won't be getting married anytime soon."

"If you think he's got an attitude now, wait until he gets out of jail in about five years," Cap said. "Five years of sitting in a cell, worrying if somebody is going to stick a shank into you or wants to make you their girlfriend, will give you a real attitude."

"Lonnie G was in jail once before," Earl said. "I thought when he got out he would get himself together. He was talking like he was he going to stay out of trouble."

"The problem with so many young men like Lonnie is that when they're young, they really don't know how to get their lives together," Duke said. "After a while they just give up and start talking about how they really don't care. But then when they get older and see what life has to offer, they want the same things everybody else wants: a decent job, a good home for their families, and to be able to take care of their kids. But they don't have the skills. It's got to be frustrating for them."

"He could have sure moved away from being a stickup man," Cap said. "He understood that. They say that when the cops opened the back door, he was trying to hide under some garbage."

"He's lucky the cops didn't shoot him," Earl said. "Especially if they knew he had a gun."

"Now his grandmother is praying for him,"

Cap said, "and asking everybody else to pray for that knucklehead. If he does get out of this, he's just going to be in trouble again down the line."

"You know, I don't think it's fair of you to talk about his choices," I said. "Lonnie G's not all that smart."

"Not like you," Kevin said. "You're a real brain."

"Hey, Kevin, I'm going to—" The next words got out faster than I could stop them. I turned to see if Duke had heard me, and I could see by his face that he had.

"Jimmy, why don't you go on home," Duke said. "I don't think you need to be here anymore today."

I looked over at Kevin, and he was looking away but I could see he was smirking. All I could think about was smashing his face. I got my jacket down from the coat rack and just left.

All the way home I thought about what had happened. That was the same crap that had got me into trouble in the first place. Somebody messing with me and then me getting into trouble for reacting to it. At least I didn't hit Kevin, because if I had started, they would have to put me in Alcatraz or someplace.

"You're home early, baby," Moms said.

"I don't feel so good," I said. "Think I'm going to lie down for a while."

"You coming down with something?"

"No."

I fell down across the bed and just tried to shut out everything. I was mad at Kevin, and I was mad at me, too. Not only that, but I knew I was going to have to hear Cap's mouth the next time I went to the barbershop.

I got hungry about six thirty and went into the kitchen. By then Moms was mad at me, too.

"Nice of you to come out for dinner," she said. "Do you mind if I serve you?"

"You don't have to do nothing for me," I said. I went back to my room and put the radio on. I couldn't shake off being mad. I thought about going out and apologizing, but I didn't.

About eight o'clock Moms said she was going over to her cousin's house to get her hair done.

"There's some food if you want it," she said.

When I heard the front door close, I went out into the kitchen and saw that she had left a plate of food for me. I sat at the table and started eating it. I was about halfway finished when someone knocked on the door. It was Duke.

137

"Come in."

Duke came in, and I told him Moms had gone to her cousin's house. He asked me if I thought that the language I had used in the barbershop was necessary.

"Duke, you know I don't," I said. "I'm sorry."

"I'm glad to hear that," Duke said. He put his legs straight out in front of him and crossed them at the ankles. "When you were at the shop, you said that it wasn't fair that Lonnie G had to make the same choices as everybody else because he wasn't that smart. Is that right?"

"Not everybody knows as much as you and Cap," I said. "You guys are cool and everything, and you've seen a lot. You went to college, too. Right?"

"Yes, that's right," Duke said. "But let me tell you something, Jimmy, it doesn't matter if you're smart or if you're not smart. All of us, including Lonnie G, do either one of two things. We either go through life making the choices that will make our lives what we want, or we don't make choices and deal with anything that comes along. And sometimes that 'anything' can be pretty hard. Lonnie G's no different than you and me when it comes to the choices he has to make. We've talked about reading, and Lonnie G had to decide if he was going to be a reader or not. We talked about sex, and Lonnie G had to decide what he wanted to do about that."

"I don't think Lonnie G's that smart," I said. "I'm just saying some people have an advantage. You know what I mean? The way you're putting it is that everybody has the same chance and everybody has the same choices. I just don't think that's true."

Duke rubbed his chin and shook his head. "Jimmy, if I told you that life was fair, or if I told you that everybody had the same chance, I'm sorry," he said. "But what I think is that you believe that words like democracy, and equal rights, mean something about basic fairness. What those words mean is that people can't make laws that are unfair. But when you talk about individual choices, that's something else.

"You're in school, that's a choice," he went on. "You save your money or don't save your money, that's a choice. You take care of your health, that's another choice. The choices don't have to be fair, but you still have to learn what they are and which ones you need to make. That's what it's all about. Knowing that you have choices to make, and making the best ones."

"And you don't care if it's easy for some people and hard for other people, right?" I asked.

"To be truthful, sometimes I care and sometimes I don't," Duke said. "If I didn't care at all, I wouldn't be talking to you now. But I know that my parents taught me some things that might have given me an edge over Lonnie G. That's how life is. I read about a woman who wrote a cookbook back in 1936. That cookbook made so much money that she never had to work another day in her life. Her children didn't have to work and her grandchildren didn't have to work. You can say that it's not fair that some people have that much money, and you can try to change some of the advantages if you have a mind to, but you're still going to either make the choices or be a victim."

"Yeah, I guess," I said. "And I am sorry about what I said to Kevin this afternoon."

"Kevin is making choices about what he says, and with his attitude," Duke said. "And whatever those choices are, he's going to have to live with them."

"You think it's right that somebody doesn't even have to worry about money because their grandmother wrote a book," I asked, "while somebody like Lonnie G is thinking about sticking up a grocery store just so he can get married?"

"No," Duke said, quietly. "I was raised black in a segregated society that was trying to hold black people down. I didn't think that was fair, either. But I either had to deal with it or let it deal with me. I chose to deal with it."

Before he left, Duke told me that he would have to take the time I was away from the barbershop from my pay. Sometimes I thought Duke was about the coldest dude I knew.

Peter the Grape

"It wasn't my fault! I just said I didn't want to be his woman no more if he wasn't ready to get married!" Jade, Lonnie G's girlfriend, had a high, screechy voice. "His grandmother's looking at me like I did something wrong, and I told her that it was Lonnie G who wasn't acting right."

"What did they say downtown?" Duke asked.

"The gun wasn't nothing but a plastic toy gun, so they talking about thirty-six months to sixty months if he pleads guilty," Jade said. Her screech died down a little and she was pouting.

"Well, he did commit a crime," Cap said.

"I still love him and everything, so I will wait for him," Jade said. "I told him he should try to get his GED while he's in jail. They're sending him all the way up to some jail near Buffalo. That's almost eight hours by bus and one hundred and thirty dollars round trip! I got the patience, honey, but I sure ain't got the money."

Duke said that maybe they could talk to the courts and have Lonnie G put in jail nearer his home because of his grandmother's age. Jade said that Lonnie G was doing all right, but he was depressed.

"Jail will definitely do that for you," Cap said.

Jade left, and Cap and Duke talked about how hard it was for men to get jobs once they got out of jail. Cap said it was hard for people like Lonnie G, who didn't have a high school diploma, to get a job even if he hadn't been in jail.

Me and Kevin weren't doing a whole lot of talking. Kevin did well in school and he just flat out thought his doo-doo didn't stink.

What's more, he wanted to make sure I knew it, too.

Cleaning the barbershop every day the way we did kept it looking nice. Duke had bought some old photographs, and we put them up and he said he wanted to buy some more stuff to fix the barbershop up like an old-time shop.

"Give it a little different character," he said. "Give the people something different to look at."

The telephone rang and Duke answered it. Cap was looking through a book called *The Best of the Police Gazette* and laughing at the stories. The *Police Gazette* was a newspaper that had been published about a hundred years ago, but the stories were funny.

"Here's a story about a woman who had a fight with her boyfriend and beat him up so bad he had to call the cops," Cap said. "Man, if my woman beat me up that bad, I think I would just go on and take it and keep my mouth shut."

"Okay, I got a question for you, Jimmy and Kevin." Duke hung up the phone. "Which of you has personally met a black millionaire?"

I didn't know any black millionaires and neither did Kevin. We were both shaking our heads when Mister M came into the shop, and

Duke asked him if he knew any black millionaires. Mister M said he didn't know any either.

"Well, you're going to meet one at four thirty today," Duke said. "Peter Scott is coming in to have his hair cut."

"Good gracious!" Cap slapped his thigh. "Peter the Grape!"

"Let me tell you about this guy before he gets here," Duke said. "Peter grew up on 147th Street, between Seventh and Eighth, and then his family moved to the Dunbar Houses. His mother never was married, so he was raised by her and his grandfather, who worked on the railroad. When Peter was coming up, he couldn't do a thing. Couldn't even tie his shoes right. I remember one time we were all tying our shoes so that the laces went straight across. You remember that, Cap?"

"Yeah, we didn't have no reason for it, just did it," Cap said.

"Peter couldn't get his shoelaces right if he stayed up all night," Duke went on. "He couldn't play basketball, he couldn't play baseball and Lord knows he couldn't dance. We used to call him Peter the Grape because he was about as useful as a grape."

"He sounds stupid to me," Kevin said.

"He wasn't stupid," Cap said, "but old Peter was definitely not going to give Einstein a run for his money."

"His grandfather worked on the railroad and gave Peter one of the schedules they used for railroad employees. This was a long book they used to track where the workers were," Duke said. "He also gave him a watch. It wasn't a good watch, but Peter loved it."

"Every day he used to get up and write down where he was in the morning," Cap added, laughing. "Which was home."

"Here he comes now," Duke said. He looked at the clock on the wall. It was twenty-nine minutes past four.

Peter Scott pushed the door open and came in. He was a dark, round-faced dude with a scraggly-butt mustache. He wore a light-blue jacket over a sweatshirt, camouflage pants and dirty skips. When he took off the jacket, he looked skinny but he still had him a little potbelly.

"Mr. Wilson," he said. "How are you doing?"

"I'm doing fine, Mr. Scott," Duke said. "How are you doing?"

"Well, I'm hanging in there," Peter said.

"I see you still got Cap here holding down the fort."

"You know I'm not going anywhere, Peter," Cap said. "I have to make sure the neighborhood is running right."

"You know that's the thing to do," Peter said. "Am I right after these young men?"

"You're next, Peter. This is Jimmy Lynch and this is Kevin Bracken, two young men who help me keep this place clean," Duke said. "They're fine young men."

"Well, I'm pleased to meet you boys," Peter said.

"So what are you up to these days?" Duke asked, as Peter settled into the barber's chair. "You still dealing with automobile radiators?"

"You can't go wrong with radiators," Peter said. "They got them little weak bumpers. They give real quick, and the first thing you know, you got a messed-up radiator."

"How did you get in the radiator business?" Duke asked.

"I used to work for a guy over in Jersey City," Peter said. "He used to do car repairs and he taught me a lot, because you know I didn't know a lot about fixing no cars. He could fix any kind of car and fix any part except

the radiator. We used to send the radiators all the way out to Newark.

"I had to drive the radiators out to Newark and then pick them up when they were ready to go back into the car," Peter went on. "The radiator wasn't so hard to fix, but you had to have the right tools to handle that copper and whatnot. You also had to buy the copper and do your own welding, which I could do. One day I saw a radiator company go out of business and I asked the man, a big Italian fellow, what he was going to do with his tools. He said he'd sell them to me for three hundred dollars. I bought them tools and started fixing radiators at night. I fixed them for my boss first, but then later I started fixing them for everybody. My boss just wanted me to work for him, and he'd take the money, but you know I thought I could do that for myself."

"He wanted you to be his employee and take your business for his own," Duke said.

"Yeah, yeah, that's right," Peter said. "One day he said that if I didn't work for him and just him, I was going to get fired that day. I told my boss I would think about it. There was an empty place right next door, and I went over and asked the guy if he would rent it to me. He said yes, so I just moved myself over there and set up business."

"You were in business for yourself!" Cap said.

"I did that for a while, and then I saw the most expensive thing I had to deal with was that copper. So what I did was to start buying old copper, melting it down and re-forming it," Peter said. "Then I started making good money."

"How many people you have working for you?" Cap asked.

"I got about ten fellows working in the radiator shop," Peter said.

"You come over from the shop today?" Duke asked.

"No, I got a little apartment thing going," Peter said. "You know I bought some of those buildings over on 141st Street."

"You got some buildings down in North Carolina, too," Duke said. "I remember you set up your mama down there, didn't you?"

"Yeah, that was nice," Peter said. "I was coming over from my real estate office."

Duke took the apron off of Peter and brushed away some of the loose hair on his

150

shoulders. "Peter, what was the most important advice you've ever received?" Duke asked.

"Well, I don't know what that would be," Peter said. "People give you lots of advice. Maybe what Dick Gregory said to me. You ever meet Dick Gregory?"

"No, I never did," Duke said. "Where did you meet him?"

"I was living down on the Lower East Side," Peter said. "You remember I bought that little apartment building I had to fix up?"

"Right."

"I used to go down to the track over on the east side and run a little," Peter continued. "One day I seen this guy running on the track. He wasn't running that good, but he had this real pretty running suit on. I thought I could beat him, so I ran along next to him and told him I would race him. Man, that fool could run!"

"Before he became a comedian, he was a world-class runner," Cap said.

"I didn't know that!" Peter said. "Anyway, I ran against him and he ran away from me like I was standing still. When he had run around the track and stopped, I caught up with him and asked him just how much he ran. He said when he was fasting, which meant he wasn't eating nothing, he ran three miles a day. When he was eating regular, he ran six miles a day. Whooo-ee! That was something. I told him that I thought he was very impressive. He said it only took him two hours a day to change into his running clothes, get down to the track, run, go home and take a shower. He said if I couldn't find two hours a day to do something for myself, I needed to figure out what I was living for.

"Now, that wasn't no advice because he didn't say I should do anything," Peter said. "But I remembered what he said. You know, I keep a record of my time. So I went back and looked at what I was doing for Peter Scott. You know what I mean?"

"I sure do," Duke said.

"How much I owe you?" Peter asked, checking himself out in the mirror.

"Seven fifty," Duke said. "Let me ask you, Peter, you buy anything else I should know about?"

"It ain't no big thing," Peter said. "But I did buy a small plane. But that's only because I'm going between North Carolina and New York so much. It's hard when you got business in two different states."

"I know what you mean," Duke said.

Peter Scott paid his bill and shook everybody's hand, including mine and Kevin's, before he left.

"That dude is a millionaire?" Kevin asked when Peter Scott had left.

"He's a multimillionaire," Duke said. "And I think it all started with him keeping careful track of his time in that book his grandfather gave him."

"Okay, we need to deal with this," I said. "Duke, your whole rap is about taking charge of your life and getting into something positive, right?"

"More or less," Duke said.

"Not more or less," I said. "That's what you've been saying all along. But that guy is a millionaire, right?"

"He's probably got five or six million by now," Duke said.

"But it sounds to me like he just kind of lucked into it," I said.

"He did the right thing," Cap said, "No matter how he got to it. The right thing is the right thing."

"Peter's got two things going for him,"

Duke said. "He's got his life and his time organized, and he's active. I'll bet there were fifty guys working in the same garage he was working in who saw the chance to make some extra money fixing radiators, but Peter was the only one who did anything about it."

"If I was a millionaire, I would have you coming to me to cut my hair," Kevin said to Duke.

"Peter could have somebody coming to him and cutting his hair and doing his nails and anything else he wanted," Duke said. "But he doesn't have anything to prove. He's just a brother from the hood who got himself together early on and took care of business."

Okay, so all the way home I was thinking about Peter, and it bothered me. He might be a millionaire, but like Kevin was saying, he sure didn't look like anything special. And in a way I knew I didn't think he should be no millionaire because I wanted him to look and act sophisticated, which he did not. And all the time I'm thinking this, I was checking me out thinking what I was thinking. I bet that was what Duke did all the time.

When I got home, Bailey was there. Moms said that Uncle Gilbert had brought her by and

she was going to stay with us until the weekend because there was a reunion of the 369th up in Albany that Uncle Gilbert had gone to.

"Which means that I have to walk the little rat," I said.

"Oh, Jimmy, it won't kill you to walk the dog," Moms said. "And I think it's about time to walk her now."

I took Bailey out and walked her twice around the block and then sat on the stoop for a while.

"Bailey, count to ten!" I said.

Bailey barked once.

"Two!" I said.

Bailey barked again.

"Three!"

Bailey barked again. I just looked at her for a while. Then she barked again. I wondered if the stupid dog thought she was teaching me.

Sister Smith on a God Tip

I woke up Saturday morning and I heard this deep voice coming from the other room. My door was closed, so I couldn't hear it too clearly, but I thought it was Duke. It was nine thirty and I wondered why Duke was there so early. I got up, pulled on my pants and sneakers and went out to the bathroom. That's when I saw it wasn't Duke but Sister Smith.

Sister Smith is my mother's aunt. She's tall and thin, wears plain glasses and looks a little like a man.

"Good morning, James," Sister Smith said.

"Good morning, ma'am," I answered.

"Your mother is telling me about how good you are doing down at that barbershop," Sister Smith said.

"You ought to hear some of the deep stuff he's talking about," Moms said.

"So tell me what you've learned." Sister Smith's voice was deeper than mine.

"I have to go to the bathroom," I said.

"I'll be here," Sister Smith answered.

I don't think Sister Smith ever enjoyed anything. If she was in the room by herself and a smile sneaked in, she'd beat it up and pee on it. If she had a motto, it would be "If God don't get you, I will!"

I had to be careful about what I said to her, because I knew I could spend all morning in one of her lectures. I washed up slow, letting the water run real loud so she would think I was washing, not stalling.

When I got out of the bathroom, she was sitting with her long fingers wrapped around a cup of coffee. Moms asked me if I wanted some toast and eggs, and I said I did.

"I'll go make it," Moms said, abandoning her beloved son, "while you tell Sister Smith about some of your conversations with Duke."

I turned and looked at Sister Smith as Moms left the room.

"So what are you talking about down at the barbershop?" Sister Smith asked.

"Mostly about how you have to choose what you do in life," I said.

Sister Smith leaned forward as far as she could and looked around real sneaky like before she spoke. "And you didn't know that, honey?" she said. "Is that what you're telling Sister Smith?"

"I knew it in a way," I said. "But I didn't know I had to do it every day. I didn't know how many choices there were."

"That's Duke Wilson down at the barbershop?"

"You know him?" I asked.

"I've known him all my life," Sister Smith said. "Used to go to dances with him when I was in my dancing days. I often see Duke walking past the church, or sitting in his automobile on a Sunday afternoon cruising down the avenue. And I'm very interested in finding out what Mr. Wilson has to say about God Almighty."

"We don't talk about God that much," I

said, knowing I was headed for deep water. "Mostly, like I said, we talk about choices."

"And do you talk about choosing the ways of the Lord over the ways of the world?" Sister Smith asked.

"I know enough to choose what's right," I said. "And that's why Duke is talking to us."

"But does Mr. Duke Wilson call the name of God when he's speaking to you?"

"No, ma'am," I said. "But he said I should go to church."

"And you and he are choosing not to talk about God," Sister Smith went on. "Is that what Sister Smith is hearing?"

"Maybe we just haven't got to God yet," I said.

"So God has to wait his turn?"

"No, ma'am."

"So what choices are you and Duke Wilson making?"

"Mostly we're just going over the idea that everybody has to make choices and, you know, participate in their own lives," I said. "Like if you don't read, then you're making a choice not to read. If you have sex, you're making a choice to have sex and then you got to check out whatever."

160

"Whatever. I see. So first you talk about reading, and then you talk about sex." Sister Smith was counting on her fingers. "What other choices are you making down at the barbershop?"

"To be successful," I said.

"When you're talking about reading, are you talking about reading the Bible?"

"That's like, your choice," I said, glad that I was thinking fast. "You can choose to read the Bible if you want to do that."

"I'm not going to ask you what you choose to read," Sister Smith answered. "But I will ask you just where in this house is your Bible?"

"I know we have one," I said.

"So do you think God might be upset—just a little, mind you—that He is being ignored?"

"I'm not ignoring God," I said.

"Just choosing to think more about reading and sex and success?"

"I think God knows I'm headed in the right direction."

"I bet you feel funny sitting there hearing me talk about God, don't you?" Sister Smith said. "Me putting God all up in your face when you just want to eat your breakfast and get this old black woman out of your hair?"

"I don't feel funny," I lied.

"Yes, you do, honey," she said. "And that's all right. Don't be in no hurry to jump on God's bandwagon just because riding is easier than walking. You can think on it for a while, and it won't hurt to pray on it, either. You know, God is the one who really wants you to be all that you can be. He gave you such wonderful gifts—you're healthy, young and strong. You got eyes to see around you and ears to listen. And after you see and hear what's going on, you can use that mind He gave you to put it all together and do right for yourself. Now isn't that a blessing?"

"Yes, ma'am."

"Now let me ask you something," she said. "When I leave out of here, are you going to say, 'There goes that crazy Bible-talking lady?'"

"No, ma'am."

"Yes, you will," Sister Smith said, picking up her purse. "You're just being polite. It's good to see young boys with some manners. It would be even better to see you getting serious about your spiritual life. Now when you go and see Mr. No Dancing Duke, because he couldn't dance, see what he says about that."

When Sister Smith left, I asked Moms how

come she had deserted me when I needed her most.

"I think we all need God in our lives, Jimmy," Moms said. "But I would rather have Sister Smith on your case than on mine."

That was cold. Real cold.

Bobby Brown

I got to the shop as Duke was just finishing a customer's hair. The customer paid his bill in change and was apologizing for all the nickels and dimes he had, but Duke said it wasn't a big thing.

"Money is money," he said.

The customer left and Duke went over to where Cap was sitting behind the checkerboard. Cap's eyes were closed, and I watched Duke move one of Cap's pieces before making his own move. Then he went to the barber's chair, sat down and reclined the chair.

164

"Cap, it's your move!" Duke called out.

Cap opened his eyes, wiped his mouth with his fingertips and then looked over the board. After a while he pushed one checker forward with his finger. "Looks like you got me," he said.

Duke looked at the board from where he sat, nodded and then went over and took one of Cap's men. Cap chuckled to himself, then took three of Duke's men to win the game.

It was almost four o'clock, and Kevin was late. Sometimes it was easier for me to talk to Duke and Cap when Kevin wasn't around, so I gave it a try.

"Say, Duke, suppose someone asked you for advice," I said. "And you knew the person really didn't have much of a shot in life, right? What would you say?"

"There wouldn't be any use in my talking to him," Duke said. "Because if he doesn't have any chance in improving his life, it means he's dead and he wouldn't hear me anyway."

"Yo, Duke, I don't mean to be disrespectful or nothing," I said. "But when you're talking about people doing things with their lives, you're usually talking about people who have a lot of things going for themselves. But suppose a brother didn't have anything going on, what would you say?"

"Tell me about this hopeless case," Duke said.

"Okay, there's this guy in my math class," I said. "Yesterday the teacher was all over him. Bobby's a little guy, and that's why the teacher doesn't mind getting on him so hard. I don't think the teacher would be throwing that much stuff my way."

"Right, because you would exercise that famous temper of yours and get thrown out of class right away!"

"So what did the teacher say?" Cap asked.

"He said the only way Bobby wouldn't flunk out of school was if he dropped out," I said, remembering how mad it had made me to hear it. "And then he ran this rap about how he would see Bobby one day on television getting into the back of a police car or maybe standing on a corner asking for spare change."

"The teacher said that in front of the class?" Cap asked.

"Yeah. I was thinking of going up to him

and knocking him out," I said. "But I didn't want to get Duke upset."

"And what do you think about this young man?" Duke asked. "What did you say his name was?"

"Bobby Brown," I said. "He's an okay dude, but his grades are, like, not even on the page. He's, like, just putting in time till he gets paroled from school. Then he's got to deal with the street thing, and like everybody says, you might not be ready for Scuffle City, but Scuffle City is ready for you."

"Duke, is that what you're always running your mouth about?" Cap asked.

"I guess so. At least that's what Youngblood here believes," Duke said. "Let me get this straight, now. Your teacher says this Bobby has no chance in life, and you agree with your teacher. So the clear course of action for Bobby is to go on and die?"

"I'm not saying that," I said. "But I feel like I should say something to the guy or think of something he can do. Something! You know what I mean?"

"Yes, I know what you mean," Duke said. "Sometimes it seems that there's a whole army of young boys in that same position. Way behind in their schoolwork, getting pushed to the next level and don't have a clue to what to do with themselves.

"The problem is that for whatever reason, they've been spectators in their own lives. They go to school because they have to go, or because their parents make them go, but they just pass the time of day. Then one day they look around and realize there's a big foot out there in what you call Scuffle City ready to kick them smack-dab in the hind parts. Then they either go through a game of 'I don't care' or they go around being mad at the world."

"You got some good-doing rules for them?"

Duke looked at himself in the mirror, decided he needed a shave and started putting lather on his face. "The first thing they have to do is figure out how long they're going to live," he said. "If they figure to die within the next few days, they should just kick back and relax. But if they figure to live, say, ten or fifteen years more, then they know they have to make a move. To start making a move, you have to figure out where you are. If you're way back and you have a lot of ground to make up, then you got to go make it up. You can't go around pretending that you're right up there with the next guy when you know you're not."

"That's not really up to him—it's up to the teacher," I said. "That's what they're paying the teacher for. Bobby's only a kid. He's sixteen."

"Jimmy, there comes a time in your life when you realize your life is your responsibility," Duke said, hitting the strop with his razor. "If somebody doesn't do their job and give you what you need, it's still your life. If somebody steps on your toes or takes the bread out of your basket, it's still your life. The teacher should offer to help him, but if he doesn't, Bobby still has to live. So the first thing he needs to do is to get up off his attitude and figure out where he needs to go.

"If I was that young man I would look for a mentor, somebody who could point him in the right direction and tell him how to get in the struggle."

"Yeah, well, it's easy to run your mouth about, but it ain't really that easy."

"You can say that again," Duke said. He was shaving, looking in the mirror that ran along the back wall.

"And anyway, the way you're putting it, the

first thing Bobby has to do is to show lame and then hope he can cop some slack on a humble, right?"

"He don't want to be embarrassed," Cap called out.

"Jimmy, it takes a big man to admit he needs some help," Duke said. "To let everybody look at you and know you have some areas of weakness. I see people come right into this bar-bershop that can't hardly read. That hurts them, their families, their living conditions. But they're protecting that pride thing. Imagine how much better they would feel if they just went on and learned to read."

"Yeah, I guess. But what am I going to tell Bobby if I see him tomorrow?"

"Tell him that no matter how he got where he got, it's up to him to move to a better place," Duke said. "That's for starters. Then you tell him to look around for somebody who can give him some good advice, somebody to mentor him. Then you tell him that he's got to start the catching-up process whether he does it in a hurry or whether it takes him ten years. He knows where he's at, and he has to make a choice of staying there or moving on. Then tell him you're on his side. That's important, too."

170

"I don't know if I want to tell him all that," I said. "I don't want to sound like a teacher."

"We all know that wouldn't do," Duke said. He finished shaving and put on some cologne. Then he lifted my chin like he was looking to see if I needed a shave. Then he said something weak about how if I stood in the wind long enough, I might never have to shave. Very weak.

Duke didn't say anything about Kevin not showing up and neither did Cap, which pissed me off. Duke and Cap were probably talking about Kevin not showing up after I left. I could have handled the conversation, even if they didn't think so. I thought they were treating me different from Kevin. I didn't like it but I didn't speak on it.

I got home and Moms asked me if I wanted to eat out, and I said sure. We went to a restaurant on Malcolm X Boulevard, and Moms pulls this thing like I was her date or something. I told her not to carry it too far, though, because I didn't have any cash to pay the bill.

I told her about Bobby, too, and what had gone down in school with the teacher getting up in his face. When I told her what Duke had said about it, she said she agreed with him.

"That's because both of you are at that age," I said.

"Could be," Moms said. "You going to talk to Bobby tomorrow?"

"Yeah," I said. "Maybe."

Change

When I got to the shop, Kevin wasn't there. Again. I knew something was up with him. Duke and Cap not talking about something can be as loud as them talking about it.

"Jimmy, did I ever tell you about the time I put fertilizer on my upper lip to try to raise a mustache?" Cap asked.

"Fertilizer? Isn't that toxic or something?" I asked.

"Not the kind of fertilizer my granddaddy was using," Cap said. "It was pure horse manure."

That cracked me up completely. I could

just imagine Cap putting some horse doo-doo on his lip. "You grow anything?"

"I grew wiser and stinkier," Cap said. "That's happened to me a lot in my life. Lucky for me I'm a little wiser than I am stinky. How you doing today, young man?"

"Not too good," I said. "I got into a thing with my moms this morning. She woke up in one of her moods. She ran down the whole nine on me. How she wasn't appreciated. How nobody cared how hard she worked. How she was being taken for granted. I was just hoping she wasn't going to get into how she wasn't going to be appreciated until she died, and then she asked me if I knew the first time she would be missed."

"And what did you say?" Cap asked.

"I said, 'When you're dead,' and she started crying all over the place."

"And you didn't know that was the wrong thing to say?" Duke turned his head and looked at me sideways.

"I knew it just as I heard it coming out my mouth," I said, "but then it was too late to get it back in."

"You know why you said it?" Duke asked.

"Why?"

"Because you're stupid!"

"Thanks for sharing that with me," I said. "But now I got to get back in with Moms somehow."

"I'll give you an advance against your salary," Duke said. "You can buy her some flowers."

"Then she's going to know I'm trying to get back on her good side," I said.

"Isn't that the point?"

I started to answer, but then Duke handed me the glass cleaner and pointed toward the mirror. The way I figured it, if I stayed in the shop for two more years, I would wipe my way right through that mirror.

"Man oh man oh man!" Bert Moody came into the shop huffing and puffing. The shirt he was wearing was soaked with sweat. He took off his hat and sank into the chair next to Cap. "Life ain't right! You hear me?"

"Why don't you tell me what's wrong," Cap said, "so I know if I need to be running or praying."

"Cap, I am so tired of living from hand to mouth. I live in a hot apartment with no air conditioning, no cable and without anything that anybody can say is the good life. I am up to my neck in bills, and now my wife is talking about getting violin lessons for our daughter," Bert said. "Now where am I going to get the money for some violin lessons? Marsha's running her mouth about when she married me, I wanted the finer things in life. Heck, I still want the finer things in life but I ain't got no finer-things money. What I need is a change in my life."

"I hear what you're saying," Duke said.

"What I need is a good Christian man to come down to the bank and cosign for me so I can get me a bill-consolidating loan," Bert said. "You get one of them, and instead of making nine or ten payments you just make one easy payment. That way you get a chance to get back on your feet."

"You don't need a Christian," Cap said. "What you need is a fool. If the bank don't want to loan you the money because they don't think you're going to pay them back, why should anybody else sign for it?"

"Yeah, you got a point, my brother, but you talking about the old Bert. When I get through this mess, I'm going to be a changed man." Bert was wiping the sweat from the back of his neck. "I'm going to get my thing together and move out to the 'burbs. That's what I need, some 'burbs, because this city living is messing me around."

"You think it's city living that's messing you around?" Duke asked.

"Yeah, man. Too much stuff going on in the city, and it all costs money," Bert said. "If I lived in the 'burbs, I wouldn't have a problem and I wouldn't be feeling this bad all the time. I ain't just got the blues, the blues got me."

"That's the only change you going to make?" Duke asked. "Moving to the suburbs?"

"You don't need to change your whole life," Bert said. "All you need is to change what's messing you around. And it's being associated with all the low-lifes around here that's ruining me. That's why I thought if I could get somebody willing to give a brother a hand, things would go all right for me. I just need somebody to go through the formality, because I'm definitely going to tighten up the payments myself."

"Don't waste your time just sitting there," Cap said. "If you looking for somebody to go to the bank with you, you'd better get out of here and start looking."

"Cap, you are a hard man," Bert said.

"That's what's wrong with this city, people are getting harder than the sidewalks. You hear that? Harder than the sidewalks!"

Bert left, but not before he stopped and gave Cap a mean look. What I noticed, though, was that even though Bert looked like he was mad, he didn't mess with Cap too much.

"Jimmy!" Duke called out my name and I jumped.

"What?"

"Bert said he was going to change," Duke said. "You think people can change?"

"Yeah, if they really want to change," I said.

"What do you think, Cap?"

"It's hard for me to use my experience on this one," Cap said. "Because working in the court system, you see a lot of people who don't change. I've seen fellows crying and begging some judge for a chance to stay out of jail and swearing to God that they would change. If they got a chance and didn't wind up in jail, I'd see them in six months to a year, begging the same beg and crying the same salty tears."

"I think there's people who want to change," Duke said, "but they don't know what they want to change. Take old Bert, for example. What my man wants to change most is the way he feels.

He wants his wife to be happy with him, he wants his daughter to be happy with her violin lessons, he wants some air conditioning so he'll be cool. He wants to feel good."

"Nothing wrong with wanting to feel good," I said.

"That's true, but sometimes it gets in the way of changing, if that's what you need to do," Duke said. "You know, we all develop life strategies, little things we do to get us through our lives and make us feel good about ourselves. Bert likes to spend money on things. Sometimes you see people want to have nice things to wear."

"Like gold chains, or the tightest sneakers," I said.

"Now you got it," Duke said. "And if you need those things to make you feel good about yourself, it's hard to give them up. You ever see a guy in a bad situation and he acts like he just doesn't care?"

"Lots of times," I said.

"Well, acting like he doesn't care is a lot easier for him than admitting that his situation is eating him up inside," Duke said. "His attitude becomes a kind of mask that he keeps even though it hurts him. What he needs to do is to stop dealing with how he feels today and figure out how he can change the way he's living so he can create a better situation for himself."

"Yeah, you got some good-doing words," I said. "But you just can't just hop up and change your life like that. You make it sound easy."

"But I know it's not," Duke said. "I know some things are just plain hard to do. I also know that hard don't equal bad. You have to ask yourself this question: In five years, where will I be with this attitude, and do I really want to be there?"

"What happened with that boy you were talking about the other day?" Cap asked. "He sounded like he needed some changes. You say anything to him?"

"Yeah, I told him some things about him needing some help and how he had to admit it to himself," I said.

"And what did he say?"

"He copped an attitude and told me he wasn't my woman and for me to watch my mouth," I said. "But then later on he came over and said everything was cool."

"And what did you say to that?" Duke asked.

"Nothing—he made me mad! I told him *later* for his jive self!"

"Let me get this straight." Duke had taken out a can of polish and was polishing his shoes with a small brush. "So you talked to him to help him and he got mad, and then he got his act halfway together but by that time you got mad because he was mad at you, right?"

"Yeah."

"When your generation takes over the world, who you going to run it with?" Duke asked.

"It won't be with no Bobby Brown."

Kevin makes the scene. He comes into the shop looking like the bad guy in a karate flick, the one who always ends up getting knocked out first. He threw his jacket on a chair and grabbed a broom and started sweeping the floor.

"Good afternoon, sir," Cap said.

"Yeah, good afternoon," Kevin said.

"You come in here with an attitude that's ugly and with a mad look on your face," Cap said. "What I want to know is, does the ugly part have the upper hand or does the mad part have the upper hand?"

"Whatever," Kevin said.

If you were mad or something, Duke and Cap would just leave you to yourself, and they left Kevin to grumble by himself and started talking about whether Mike Tyson could have beat Joe Louis and naturally they all said no way. I don't know how they could switch conversations like that.

"So what happened?" I asked Kevin when we left the shop. I headed west with him even though I didn't live in that direction.

"I failed the drug test, and my social worker started talking about how I needed some discipline and maybe I should go into the juvenile detention program," Kevin said.

"You did *what*?"

"It was no big thing," Kevin said.

"You were smoking weed again?"

"Drop it," he said.

"Yeah, sure."

Uncle Gilbert came over with his little rat dog. He and Moms ran their mouths about how good the neighborhood used to be and how clean it was and how everybody always got along.

"You didn't have to worry about locking your doors all the time," Moms said.

"We didn't have nothing much to steal anyway," Uncle Gilbert said. That cracked me up and I laughed, but neither Moms nor Uncle Gilbert could figure out the joke.

We ate in the living room and watched one of those real-crime stories. Just when they got to a point where they were chasing this dude in the projects, the phone rang. It was Duke.

"I just wanted to call and say that life isn't as hard as it might sound," he said. "You looked a little discouraged when you left the shop today."

"I wasn't really discouraged or nothing," I said. "But I know there's talking and then there's doing. Talk is easy and doing is hard."

There wasn't an answer for a while and I thought Duke had hung up, but then he spoke. "It gets easy once you realize that life is good and the hard work is all worthwhile."

I told Moms why Duke had called and ran down the whole bit about change. She said I was going to know a lot more than she did. Uncle Gilbert started in about how a tiger couldn't change his spots.

"A tiger doesn't have spots," I said. "They got stripes."

"That's why they can't change their spots!"

Both Uncle Gilbert and Moms thought that was funny. I got this vision in my head of the olden days with everybody sitting around telling a bunch of weak jokes and cracking themselves up. I don't know if I could have survived the olden days.

I also thought about Kevin smoking weed again and got a little mad about it. Actually I felt worse for Duke and Cap and Mister M than I did for Kevin, because they were the ones who were going to feel bad.

Froggy Goes A-Courting

"I want you to cut me an F in the back of my head and maybe an S on one side," Froggy Smith told Duke as he settled into the barber's chair.

"I think you should go for just one of your initials," Duke said. "It'll look more fashionable."

"Okay," Froggy said, "do the F. "

Froggy was built like a football player. He was over six feet tall, and had a long, narrow head, gold teeth in the front of his mouth and designer nails. He was called Froggy because he had this real gravelly kind of voice. Duke asked him how he had been doing.

"Man, everything is cool," Froggy said. "I got my thing together, wrapped tight and in the light. You know I got a new woman?"

"That sounds good," Duke said.

"Woman loves me to death. Last week she bought me a gold chain, some English leather shoes and an ivory-handled walking stick that's nearly as slick as me."

"A walking stick?" Cap looked up from his newspaper. "You going lame or getting to be a dandy?"

"I'm still handy so I must be a dandy," Froggy said. "I saw the stick in the window, and I said I liked it because it was imported from Africa. You know I'm into a black thing."

"Yeah, well, that's right good," Duke said. He was using the electric clipper to put Froggy's F in the back of his head.

"My old lady bought it soon as she got paid."

"She must love you a lot," Duke said. "Where did you meet her?"

"She came up to Green Haven when I was doing a little time up there," Froggy said. "They got this program where Christians and other folks come up and sing their little songs and stuff on Sundays. She seen me and asked me if I was cool with the Lord. Everybody knows I'm down with God. So I told her how I loved to go to church and everything. I used to belong to that little church on 115th Street across from the supermarket.

"Then Dorothy, that's my girl's name, said I was blessed even though I was in the slam. We started writing back and forth and I told her I'd like to look her up when I got out. I only had a calendar and a half to go, and when I got out I busted on up to her crib, and me and her been tight every since."

"What were you in Green Haven for?" Cap asked.

"I got jacked up for shoplifting," Froggy said. "I was getting me a five-finger discount at a raggedy little shop on 14th Street and they got me on the surveillance cameras. A shop that small needs to be putting its money in some advertising. They didn't need no cameras, because their stuff wasn't that tough in the first place."

"So what are you doing now?" Duke asked. He gave Froggy the mirror so he could see his F.

"I got me a little job with a cleaning company, but I might have to give it up because I can't stand too much dust," Froggy said. "I'm thinking about getting into the insurance business."

"Upward and onward," Cap said.

"Yeah. Yeah. You know Dorothy wants me to go back to school, and I'm thinking about that, too."

"Well that sounds real good, Froggy." Duke put some tonic on Froggy and used his whisk broom to brush off any hair that had fallen on his shoulders.

"They sent you to Green Haven the first time out?" Cap asked.

"That was the first time I was in Green Haven," Froggy said. "And to tell you the truth, I like that place a lot better than Rikers Island, New Jersey Correctional over in Kearney or any of them places, because the food is better. They serve a balanced diet up in Green Haven."

"That's important," Duke said.

Froggy paid his bill and left, but not before holding up one of his nails next to a gold tooth as he checked himself out in the mirror.

"He thinks he looks sharp!" Cap said.

"Now we're going to hear Duke's critique," Kevin said. "And seeing my man Froggy, this could take all day."

"You know what Froggy reminds me of, Cap?"

"What's that, Duke?"

"He reminds me of the monkey that died and went to heaven," Duke said. "He met Saint Peter at the gate and Peter gave him a list of sins and asked him if he had done any of them. The monkey looked the list over, shook his head sadly and said that there were three sins he had missed, and as soon as he had them under his belt he'd be back. Saint Peter told the monkey that if he committed more sins he could never get into heaven. The monkey looked at the list, looked over Saint Peter's shoulder into heaven and decided he'd go on back to Earth to have a good time. Not every monkey, or everybody, wants to go to heaven."

"Whoa. How come Froggy gets away with what he does and me and Kevin don't?" I asked. "If we talked like Froggy did, we'd get a long lecture."

"Some people are looking to make the most of their lives. They may need some help, but they're hoping for something better," Duke said. "And then you have people like Froggy, who will adjust to whatever life throws their way, as long as it doesn't mean any work for them. You go up to Green Haven, or any other prison, and you'll find some young men struggling to turn their lives around and some who just settle into a cell and start worrying about what time they serve supper."

"How come you're not talking to Froggy about getting his act together?" Kevin asked. "You gave up on him?"

"It's a funny thing—humans are the most adaptable animals on the planet," Duke said. "You can take a man from the heat of the Equator and put him in the Arctic, and he'll adapt to it. You can take him from the mountains and put him in the desert and he'll deal with it. All that's good. But people also adapt their minds. You see a person in a bad position and think he should be struggling to raise himself out of it, and instead of that he simply adapts to it. And when they adapt like that there's not a lot you can do about it."

"I don't agree with that," I said.

"Do tell!" Cap slapped his big, fat hand on

his thigh. "Youngblood does not agree! Hitch a lip up to your brain and run it by me real quick."

"You're always talking about how the worst thing you can do is to let your life slide without taking care of it," I said. "So how can you just watch Froggy mess up his life and shrug it off?"

"You're right," Duke said. "I should be speaking about Froggy and all the people you see around the neighborhood who have just settled into their lives and have given up being part of their own success."

"You're saying he doesn't want anything more from life?" I asked.

"I still think he's stupid," Kevin said.

"I think Froggy is the kind of young man who sees a better life out there," Duke said. "But when that better life involves more struggle and more hard work than he wants to take on, he just wiggles his shoulders and tells himself how much he likes the life he has. He's found the path of least resistance and decided it's not that bad."

"I still don't know," I said. "Maybe nobody told him the right stuff. You know what I mean?"

"Or maybe he didn't believe it when he heard it," Duke said. "But one thing you can bet on is that there's a separation between what Froggy knows to be the right thing to do and what Froggy knows is going to make him feel good."

Kevin kept going on about how stupid Froggy was, and most of the stuff he said was true and kind of funny, too. But I kept thinking about Bobby Brown, and how people put him down the same way Kevin was putting down Froggy.

I hung around the barbershop until after Kevin and Cap left.

"Thought I was going to have to deal with you again," Duke said.

"You want me to leave?"

"No, I want to talk with you and hear what you have to say." Duke was getting ready to lock up for the night. "I see what we were saying about Froggy bothered you."

"You've been saying that the way a lot of people mess up their lives is by being spectators instead of taking care of business, right?"

"Yeah."

"Well, I've been thinking that sometimes it's really hard not to be a spectator, because you really don't know what to do," I said. "But you don't go around running off at the mouth about being confused or nothing because most people don't care anyway. So you put up a front. You come up with something to say. So maybe you say you just don't care, or maybe you just say 'I'll take care of business later.'"

"Or you're going to play ball in the NBA even if you know you probably won't make it," Duke said, checking the locks on the shop door.

"You can't understand that?" I asked.

"Jimmy, I can understand it," said Duke. "But I know that sooner or later Froggy is going to reach a point in his life where fronting doesn't help. Then he's going to be faced with a choice of dealing with his life in a different way, or getting used to whatever comes his way."

"Duke, whatever answers you come up with, you don't come up with nothing easy, man."

"But is all this talking back and forth worth it?" Duke asked.

"I don't know right now," I said. "I'll let you know in about fifteen years."

"Good enough," Duke said. "Good enough."

Kevin Screws Up

"Jimmy. Jimmy. Wake up." Moms was shaking my shoulder and calling my name.

"What's the matter?" I asked, trying to get my head together.

"Duke just called," she said. "Kevin's been arrested. He wants us to go down to the precinct."

"What?"

She repeated what she had said, but it was still hard to believe. I got up and went to the bathroom, rinsed with mouthwash and looked at myself in the mirror. I was standing, so I knew I was awake. The little clock we keep in the bathroom said fifteen minutes past eleven. I got my clothes on and was tying my sneakers when Moms came into the kitchen.

"Duke says if his people show up at the station, the police will know that we care for Kevin," she said.

"What was he arrested for?"

"I don't know," Moms said. "Maybe Duke mentioned it and maybe he didn't. It really got me upset when he called. We can get the bus down to the police station."

"A Hundred and Thirty-fifth Street?" I asked.

"Yes."

The 135th Street police station was always busy. A lot of the cops who worked there played ball or worked out in the YMCA down the street. We took the bus and were downtown in a few minutes. Moms went to the desk sergeant and told her that we were friends of Kevin Bracken, who had been arrested.

"He's seventeen," she said.

The sergeant looked at the large book on his desk, then said that Kevin's family was talking with the arresting officers and we could have a seat.

There were about fifteen people inside the waiting room. Two guys about my age sat on a yellow couch against the wall. One of them had blood on his shoulder that had seeped through his shirt. The guy with him kept saying that they didn't have anything to worry about, but I knew by the way they were acting that they had a lot to worry about. I wondered if they had anything to do with Kevin. A heavyset woman in a housecoat and slippers sat in a chair in the corner. She was crying and rocking back and forth. The little girl with her leaned against her arm and looked at us with wide eyes.

Cap showed up, and he sat next to Moms and patted her hand. Moms asked him if he knew why Kevin had been arrested and Cap shook his head. He didn't look much in the mood for conversation, and Moms didn't push it. Neither did I.

I looked around the waiting room and it was all about sad, all about being in trouble. I thought that this was what Duke wanted to keep us away from. This. This waiting room, this precinct, this situation. The whole thing sucked.

We waited for almost twenty minutes before Duke came through the door. Kevin came behind him with his parents. Kevin had his head down. I felt really bad for him. I didn't want to stare at him, but I couldn't move my eyes away. His eyes were red, and I thought the side of his face might be swollen. His shirt wasn't buttoned right, either, and I wondered what that was all about. Had they made him undress?

Kevin's parents and Duke began talking quietly. Mostly Duke was talking, and Kevin's mother.

"Yo, man, you okay?" I asked Kevin.

He tightened his mouth and mumbled something that could have been "Yeah." I grabbed his arm and gave it a little squeeze to let him know I was there for him, and he patted it. Me and Kevin really weren't all that tight, but it still made me feel bad to see him jammed up.

Kevin's father thanked us all for coming down, and Cap said that he'd give a lift to anybody who needed one. He took Kevin and his parents home, and me and Moms went with Duke. Soon as we got into the car, I asked Duke what Kevin had been charged with.

"The charge is possession," Duke said. It was night, and the lights from passing cars ran across Duke's dark face. "That's not that bad. It's serious, but the officer said he might not even go through a trial, just be given probation.

"His parents are pretty upset, as you would expect," he went on.

I could tell that Duke was upset, too. I wanted to ask him some more questions, but Moms started going on about what a nice young man Kevin was, and by the time she had finished that, Duke had pulled up in front of our house.

"What's going to happen now?" I asked after I got out of the car.

"He's got a court date early next week," Duke said. He left it there.

At home I lay in bed and thought about what had happened. It didn't seem like Kevin had done that much, but it looked like it could blow his whole set big-time. Moms came in and sat on the bed with me for a while. I knew she was looking for something deep to say, and I was, too, in a way, but we didn't come up with anything.

"How do you feel about Kevin?" I asked her.

"My heart bleeds for him, and for his parents," she said.

I went to sleep thinking about how cool Duke had been.

Kevin had been arrested Thursday night. When I got to the shop Friday, only Cap and Mister M were there. Cap said that Duke had gone with Kevin and his dad to see an attorney. Kevin's court date was Tuesday at noon, and I hoped he would be in school Monday, but he wasn't. He didn't come to the shop, either.

When Duke walked into the shop, I asked him if he thought it would be cool if I called Kevin at home, and Duke said it was a good idea.

I called Kevin from the shop, and his mother said he was asleep. It was a little after four, and I couldn't figure out why he would be asleep at that time, so I figured he just didn't want to talk to me, but a few minutes later he called. I asked him if he wanted to go out for a soda or something, and he said he would meet me in the park if I could get away from the shop.

I got to the park before Kevin, and for a while I thought he wasn't going to show. But then I saw him coming past the playground. He was wearing a sweatshirt with a hood, and he had the hood up. When he sat down he was looking bad, like maybe he hadn't been sleeping for a couple of days.

"I guess you want to know what happened?" he said.

"If you want to talk about it," I said.

"Me and Eddie were sitting on the steps that night." Kevin spoke softly. "Then Akbar came over and asked us if we needed anything. You know Akbar?"

"Light skin, got a scar on his cheek?"

"Yeah, that's him. He asked us if we needed anything, and Eddie asked him what he had and he said he had some weed and needed thirty cents for it," Kevin said. "Eddie had the money, so he copped."

"He bought thirty dollars' worth of weed?"

"Yeah. Akbar left, and me and Eddie were just sitting there when the police rolled up on us and said they had seen the deal go down."

"If Eddie bought the stuff, why did they bust you?" I asked.

"Eddie made some blunts and gave me one," Kevin said.

"He was sitting there making blunts right on the steps?"

"Don't even talk to me about how stupid the crap was," Kevin said. "Every time I think about it I just want to throw myself in front of a bus or something. That's how depressed I am. My dad keeps looking at me and asking me what's wrong with me. My mother's crying and praying and stuff, all because of me.

"You know how it was? It was like I was running the game and at the same time I wasn't running it because I wasn't taking the weight. It was easier gaming with the weed and making believe that everything was cool than telling Eddie I wasn't down with it. All of the raps we ran down at the barbershop were there, all the stuff I knew, but I still went through with it."

Some little girls were jumping double Dutch near the fence. They saw me checking them out and went through their whole number. They were pretty good, too.

"Are you like—a junkie or something?" I asked.

"No," Kevin said. "But I almost wish I was."

"Why?"

"Because with all the stuff that I know, there's no way I should be in this mess," Kevin said. "It's like I knew and I really didn't let myself know. All the stuff Duke was saying about other people just fell right back on me. I'm supposed to be smart and everything, and here I am just another black dude who's turned himself over to the system. I got to go down to the court Tuesday, and hope I can get some mercy from people who don't even know me. All they know is—"

His voice trailed off and I saw he was crying.

"You only made a little mistake," I said. "Duke said you'll probably just get probation."

"Yeah, that could happen," Kevin said. He ran his hand over his face. "But now I have to wait until Tuesday to see what my life is going to be about. I'm supposed to be so smart, and here I am stumbling my way into whatever happens."

The girls kept on playing double Dutch,

204

and some boys came over and started messing with them. They challenged the boys to jump. The boys tried it and, when they couldn't do it, started goofing on the girls.

"Look, man, you are smart," I said. "And you know what's happening. You're strong, too. This mess can make you even stronger. You got to keep on being strong and taking care of yourself. You know what I mean? I think you're going to be all right. Really."

"You know how scared I am?"

"Yeah, I think so," I said. "I'm a little scared, too."

Me saying I was scared surprised me, but when I thought about it, I knew I was. Kevin wasn't my ace, but I knew he had heard everything that had gone down at the shop, had seen all the ways that people could get themselves jived around, same as I had, and he had gone down the same road. When I was telling him to be strong, and to take care of himself, I needed to be telling myself the same thing.

What happened to Kevin got me real nervous. I thought that if it had been me, I might have done the same thing. I don't smoke anything, not even cigarettes, but I wouldn't have wanted to show lame, so maybe I would have taken the weed. And what would have been bad, besides the fact that I would have known all the things ahead of time that should have stopped me, was that I would have disappointed everybody I knew.

I couldn't wait to get to the shop Tuesday afternoon. Duke was touching up a customer's fade, and Cap was talking about how high the rents were in Harlem.

"When I was growing up, you could rent a room for two dollars a week," he said.

"You can't even get a bed in a shelter for that kind of money today," the customer said.

I hung my jacket up and started sweeping the floor. When Duke finished with the customer, I asked him what had happened at court.

"Sit down, Jimmy."

"Oh, man!"

"The best the lawyer could do for him is eighteen months in a juvenile facility," Duke said. "He'll get out in six months with good behavior. I'm still going to try to get him into a college, maybe a junior college somewhere."

"When's he going?"

"They took him this afternoon," Duke said.

Duke looked away from me. I saw his shoulders lift and fall. Then he got up and started straightening up the counter.

I looked over at Cap, and he was holding his coffee cup in his big hands.

"Kevin's young, Jimmy. It's going to be harder now, but he's still got a chance to get his life on the right road," Cap said. "It's up to him what he does with it. That's what it always ends up being, a chance to get it right."

What I wanted to ask Duke and Cap was when getting it right was going to be easy. But by now I knew what they would say. It might never get easy, but it would be a lot better than getting it wrong.

I'm almost always on time to the shop, but Bailey made me late. There's this poster on the subway about a dancing school. LEARN BALLROOM DANCING IN JUST 3 WEEKS! I got this picture in my head of me taking this stupid dog into the dancing school and signing her up for lessons. It was kind of a funny thought, but when I looked up I saw the door was just closing at 145th Street. I had to go up to 155th, cross over and wait with a bunch of nerdy-looking kids until the downtown train came.

When I got to the shop, I saw Eddie on the steps. After what happened with Kevin, it made me mad just to see his dumb butt.

"Jimmy! What's happening?"

"What you want, man?"

"I'm looking for Kevin," Eddie said. "You see him around?"

"He got sentenced to a juvenile facility last week," I said. "You didn't hear about it?"

"Yeah, yeah, it slipped my mind, man. Hey, my case comes up next month and I ain't looking at no juvenile facility. I can't be worried about Kevin." Eddie wiped some sweat off his face with his sleeve. "Look, I know this brother who has some bad CDs. You want to cop?"

"Nah, man," I said. "You ain't nothing but trouble."

"What's the matter?" he asked. "They looking for priests and recruiting from the ghetto now?"

"Yeah," I said. "They looking for priests and they recruiting me, and when they finish with me, I'm going to recruit your mama."

He said something that was seriously stupid

and went on down the street. I waited to see if he was going to look back. He did, and that made me feel good because I felt I had just left his raggedy butt in the dust and he knew it.

Okay, so this new kid is in the shop now. His name is Ernesto. He said it meant "The Cat" in Spanish. I know it doesn't, because I asked Angela, who speaks Spanish, and she said it don't mean nothing but Ernesto. Anyway, when I got to the shop, Ernesto was opening a big box. He pointed at me, which is what he did sometimes instead of saying "Hello." He thinks it's fly but it ain't.

I took my jacket off. Cap and Mister M were playing checkers, and Duke was watching Ernesto opening the box.

Ernesto got the box opened and pulled out two large metal pots.

"Jimmy, do you know what these are?" Duke asked.

I looked them over. "Flower pots?" I guessed.

"Spittoons," Duke said. "All the bars and barbershops used to have them so people wouldn't spit on the floor."

"What kind of people you know go around

spitting on the floor?" I asked Duke.

"People used to chew tobacco all the time," Duke said. "When they had chewed all the flavor out of the tobacco or snuff, they'd spit it out."

"And nobody told them that was nasty?" I asked.

"It's not going to be nasty when you and Ernesto finish polishing them up," Duke said.

I had to give Duke a look behind that, but he was checking out his newspaper like he didn't even mind how I was looking at him. Me and Ernesto sat outside the shop on the step and started polishing the spit cans, which is what Ernesto called them.

"This is crap," Ernesto said. "I'd rather be in jail than messing with these old guys every day. At least if you're in jail, you can be with your homeboys. You know what I mean?"

"Ernesto, you are a hard brother. How old are you, anyway?"

"Fifteen," Ernesto said.

"When you going to be sixteen?" I asked.

"On the twelfth of August," Ernesto said. "I'm a Leo."

"Ernesto, you'd better listen to Duke and Cap and Mister M very carefully," I said.

"Because if they don't teach your dumb butt something real soon, I ain't going to let you live until the twelfth of August. You got that?"

He looked at me and said something about me having a problem.